The Coffee Shop Companion

VOLUME 2

Stephen Phillips

STAR ROSE
PUBLISHING
Follow your passion
and all else will follow.

All correspondence to the author:
Phone: 0419 668 345

ISBN: 978-0-6487858-5-9

Proudly produced by

TheBookStudio
www.thebookstudio.com.au

There is a 'Warning' attached to this book as some content may offend. If you are easily offended please don't read this book!

It may contain words like, knobhead, tibouchina, cannula, sepsis, weenis and cunning linguist. If any of these words offend you, please don't read this book or recommend it to anyone who may have very strict religious rules about blasphemy, atheism, flat earth theory, omnivores or missionary sex. Under no circumstances is a copy of this book to fall into the hands of a 'so-called' member of the Illuminati, whether a current member or a historical figure.

If you are a bit squeamish it may help you to read some of the more tragic poems in this compendium so you can begin to develop some calluses on your emotional constitution. Suck it up buttercup; there are a lot more people worse off than you.

Apologies have already been given, through an extensive legal team, to the literary world which covers almost 3.8 billion possible readers but there may be some intensely dangerous literature in this book which may shock, bore and cause narcolepsy and insomnia simultaneously. The management apologises in advance for ... alliteration, personification, sentences ending with the word 'do', accidental rhyming with the word 'smezna' and extensive overuse of Assyrian assonance.

What some people said ...

'I'm feeling a bit drowsy reading this already even though Stephen's stories are, you know, a bit pedestrian and typically as predictable as a 'Neighbours' plot.'

- Kylie Minge (Agent for Drag Bingo Stars)

'If you have an aversion to poorly punctuated or clumsily constructed clauses or alliteration then your cerebellum probably imploded after reading up to this point or you have broken out in a hideous chest rash.'

- Denis Drysdale

Most reviews have been consistent in their praise for the authors work.

'An interwoven masterpiece seamlessly portraying Stephen's truth, both past and present. Stories and poetic stanzas are either filled with witty humour or an air of melancholy that completely pulls you in to his unique writing style. The 'Drawer of Memories' is a particular favourite; meticulously descriptive, prompting readers to reminisce about the special treasures in their own lives.'

- Kirra Galway (Literary Agent)

'It felt like I could reach out and punch him really hard in the upper arm.'

- Lord Lloyd Leese of the Amateur Literary Society of Home Brewers

'There were moments when we thought he might have successfully found an ending to one of his stories.'

- National Foundation of Dali Lama impersonators

'Complete rubbish, really, who cares about memory and shit? I hope I forget everything in this book, especially the Goldy stories which didn't make me laugh and the walking story which did.'

- Author's publisher and Editor Claxton T. Applethwaite Jnr.3rd

'I use the book for a coffee coaster and it looks good on the table because it's about coffee, isn't it?'

- Anonymous big-mouthed MAFS bride from the 2024 season who is still single and still stupid!

'I was offended on several levels by the puerile schoolboy language, the lack of multi-gender romance and no mention of coffee.'

- Miriam McKenzie, President of W.O.K.E. (Wingers of Kingston Extraction)

'If there was a photo of him on the sleeve, I would have graffitied it with a moustache, pimples and missing teeth.'

- Anonymous member of author's family. (Hi Son, don't forget me in your royalties, this is Mum not your brother and sister)

'There has never been a more talented and authentic author in Australian history. No, wait, there has never been a less talented and authentic New York Times Worst-Selling author in Australian literary history.'

- Colleen Mc Cullock (Cafeteria employee at Myers Brisbane who served the author lunch when he worked in men's fashion on the third floor).

About the Author

Stephen Phillips is the author of the New York Times 'Worst Seller' *Forty Jobs in Forty Years*, which was written during the 2020 pandemic lockdowns. He was hoping to inspire people who had lost their jobs to look further afield and not be afraid to go into previously unexplored employment territory.

A subsequent lockdown publication (under his legal name Stephen Estella) was the *'Grandma Beans'* series of children's books which were illustrated by his wife Donna Estella.

He also published *'Kontiki the Crab'* in 2013 which was beautifully illustrated by Kylene Jacobs and was based on a 2008 surfing trip to the Maldives.

An overly keen (his wife's description of the old codger) and active musician and songwriter, Stephen has a passion for defending and protecting the environment (especially his own immediate 5-mile radius) and spends his spare time surfing, playing in a 12 piece Ska Band and a lesser known but more intimate four piece called 'The Moffat Beach No Stars' whose accumulated age is 267, picking up micro plastics on Kings Beach, cooking curries and taking the piss out of armchair activists ... he loves this last one.

Unnecessary Preulde

A compendium of literary snippets to entertain and enlighten coffee drinkers the world over. Short stories and poetry are captured in myriad forms including a series of short stories about a down and out unattractive middle-aged piano player who falls in love every night but never seems to nurture his relationships further than the length of a few songs and a visit to the worst bathroom in the world.

There are also a collection of beach poems based on the author's morning walks in Moffat Beach and an introspective look at memory and its inerasable influence on our futures.

'Walk the Walk' is a stream of consciousness piece about two people who discover the magic of a night journey which was unplanned but they uncover in each other a playful kindred spirit and mutual respect.

The free standing poems were initially published in a local magazine and were meant to provide a pseudo-mystical imagery for the reader to work out what its intention might be.

There is no information about how to grow, roast, grind or prepare coffee or even how to drink it correctly. It is intended as a short literary 'pick-me-up' over a morning beverage. It also contains no weight loss tips (other than laughing) and no scientific proof that reading has been proven to contribute to weight loss. However, I hope you feel better after a read. You can randomly flick to any page to start reading.

My walk was refreshing,
The wind in my face
And everyone sleeping
In their dark little space

My ankle was clicking and I counted the steps
Right up to the lighthouse, as good as it gets
Unfortunately, I couldn't wipe from my mind
The beautiful image of that angel sublime

As I turned down the hill
The wind lifted my hair
And I floated to home
With a thousand yard stare

So my study has retreated
For tonight at least
I'll try again tomorrow
To conquer that beast

In the meantime
I'll sleep in a peaceful dream
While the epitome of beauty
Drifts through every scene

Onshore winds massage my face as I stand on the cool clean sand

Strings of blue bottles strewn on the shore,
I hesitate to enter the unattractive brown slush

Bravely I wade in as magpies and butcher birds sound their
warnings behind me

The sea doesn't want me today pushing me back to the shallows

The Mullets forge on regardless, floating and flippering

No rideable swells, I slip repeatedly on take off

Deflated I emerge with strands of seaweed attached

Coffee with my two favourite girls makes everything alright

Another day begins

SEX.. YOUR EYES ARE ON THIS PAGE
- *BLOOD.. MAY FILL YOUR HEART WITH RAGE*
- *ECSTATIC.. AS A ZEALOT WHO THIRSTS FOR PAIN*
- *SOAKED.. IN A GARDEN OF SOFT RAIN*

RHYTHM.. UNEXPLAINED THAT MAKES YOU SWAY
- *LIES.. YOU ONLY REALISED TODAY*
- *WORDS.. CONNECTING THOUGHTS IN YOUR BRAIN*
- *NUMBERS.. FLOWING IN AN UNENDING CHAIN*
- *DEPTH.. OF THE COSMOS ABOVE YOUR HEAD*
- *MYSTERY.. REVEALED ONLY WHEN YOU'RE DEAD*
- *LIGHT.. BLINDING YOUR EYES IN THE DARK*
- *DARKNESS.. A PIT BARREN AND STARK*
- *WATER.. A POWER YOU CANNOT CONTROL*
- *AIR.. THE SACRED MEAT OF YOUR SOUL*
- *FIRE.. BURNING THE YEARS AWAY*
- *EARTH.. A CARBONIC SHEATH FOR DECAY*
- *FAITH.. IN A PRIVATE PART OF YOUR MIND*
- *BELIEF.. THAT YOU BE NOT UNKIND*
- *HIDDEN.. IN SECRET YOU NEVER REVEAL*
- *PROMISE.. ALWAYS TO CONCEAL*
- *ART.. EXPRESSING ALL THROUGH LOVE*
- *NATURE.. HOLDS ALOFT THE DOVE*

TRUTH.. IS SEEN BY ONE AT A TIME
- *LUST.. THE UNIVERSAL CRIME*
- *BLOOD.. MAY FILL YOUR HEART WITH RAGE*

,SEX.. YOUR EYES ARE STILL ON THIS PAGE.

Read it from the bottom to the top...

Wavy gods dance in the liquid sky

Nose bubbles escape to the surface

Exploding into the atmosphere

With a pop of light through a prism of air

Human frog above in slow motion

Unneeded land muscles flapping

Awkward sloshing on the surface

With clatter of humans drowning out

The watery peace beneath...

Breathe...

Submerge...

Silence...

Light dancing...

Sky stills...

Reflections

Take you

To

The

Surface...

Rise for a breath like a salty behemoth...

Two Ambulance officers are called to a 'roll over' on the highway.
They follow protocol and 'top to toe' the two men checking for
injuries. One is in the car; the other has been flung out some
distance and has cuts on his face.

"Can you feel this?" says the first ambulance officer to the
man thrown from the car.

"No, I can't" he replies feebly. The officer looks concerned
and squeezes further down the man's leg.

"Can you feel this?" he says calmly looking at the man's face.
He smells alcohol and looks at the other victim being treated by
his colleague in the overturned car. His brow knits in concern.

"Can you move your legs? What's your name?" says the
second Ambo. He is attempting to release the man from the
car but his patient seems lifeless and unable to move his legs.
He also smells of alcohol. Once breathing and heart rates have
been assessed to be normal the Ambos talk to each other and
get the stretcher and board for obvious spinal injury patients.
The two unfortunate victims are talking to each other from their
unceremonious positions on the ground near the steaming 'Push
Button Automatic Valiant' now heaving it's last breath beside
them.

"You right Mal?" says one.

"Yeh, I'm Ok", he chuckles. Then he starts to giggle and
his friend follows suit. The laughing escalates as the Ambos
approach with their spinal boards and gurneys.

"You know, you guys are in quite a bit of trouble; do you
need some pain relief?"

"Yeh, I do need a bit of relief", says the guy in the car a
little croaky voiced. The Ambo obliges with an effective and
appropriate pain killer and as his victim moans in relief, the

other man thrown out onto the verge of the highway starts to also call for relief. The second Ambo provides him with a dose of an appropriately approved opiate.

Then both the men begin to laugh harder as they are being carried to the Ambulance, almost hysterical. The Ambos are aware of the alcohol content on both men's breath and, the pain relief they had administered should have put both men into a submissive state to transport them to hospital. The two prone men continued to laugh and cackle but were eerily motionless.

The Ambulance officer who sat in the in the back between the two men is concerned at the frivolity both these reasonably young men were showing towards their condition and said,

"You realize", he said sincerely, "you may not be able to walk again". These are serious injuries you know." The men laughed again reeling in the euphoria of the medication and one of them turned to the Ambo and said,

"Yeh we drank tonight," He paused, then he said, "And I drove my car and I shouldn't have." Another pause; "But my car is especially made for paraplegic drivers and is a 'Push Button Automatic; I'm a paraplegic and my mate here is a quadriplegic so we were just fucking with you back there. We can't feel shit from here down and we didn't lie to you." They both laughed again and the Ambos turned off their siren, slowed down and looked at each other with a look of disbelief that only an Ambulance Officer can appreciate. The shit that happens! They were going to be fine!

(P.S The police had arrived after the men were loaded into the ambulance and weren't able to breathalyse them.)

An angel crossed my path today
She smiled at me as if to say
Everything will be okay

She disappeared with graceful moves
And left a heavenly perfume

I watched her go and she waved goodbye
And blended into the dusky sky

I breathed in deep and walked behind
And tried to keep her message in mind.

A smile appeared now on my face
When I thought of her angelic grace

I'll share the silent message round
When next I see somebody frown

I'll tell them everything will be okay
Because an angel crossed my path today

If my love is boundless and has no end
That means with you I would never have to pretend

I'd bathe in your smile and fall at your feet
The sound of your voice would make me complete

For every moment of everyday
I could breathe the same air and not want to stray

From your eloquent beauty and whimsical style
I'd spend my days happy with a permanent smile

For you are my destiny, my one and all
And I will come running whenever you call

I'll not get in your way or judge what you do
It's a mutual respect between me and you

Our life is a journey which seems somewhat brief
If someone steals your heart, let me be the thief.

GOLDY 1

Blue Eyes (Glitter Strip Chick)

She was in her thirties I guess. The overly bright pink lipstick and fake nails flagged a warning sign that she was trying to cover something up. She tried to flick her platinum dyed hair to look sexy but it just revealed the wrinkles on the back of her neck; she'd done it rough up till now and the resprayed silver stilettos looked uncomfortable. She tried to catch my eye through the fake mascaraed lashes. She had too much of her 70's blue eye shadow smeared across her lids.

The fact I had a cigar in one hand and whiskey in the other probably gave her the impression I was rich or lookin for someone. She sidled up to me and the overly sweet Liz Taylor perfume wafted through my cigar smoke and I gagged quietly trying not to look interested; I wasn't. That impressed her and she moved closer as I continued playing Tom Waits on the piano though how I did that with my hands full was even a mystery to me. I looked down and saw the stockinged ankle above the sparkly shoe and noticed the ladders trying to cover the badly shaved skin on her calf. Ewww!

"Buy a girl a drink?" she said with a smoky baritone. I nearly missed my favourite C9 chord.

"I would if there was a girl here," I said without looking up and blew cigar smoke at her hair.

"You're an ornery character," she said trying to make eye contact. I was happy it wasn't a question. The song should have finished by now but I was just noodling to avoid giving her an opening.

She reached for my whiskey and I could see the liver spots on the back of her hand.

I pretended not to notice and frankly didn't care; it was shit Johnnie Walker anyway. I played further up the keyboard to escape the inevitable and when I got to the end note I stood in one fluid motion and walked straight into the men's room without looking back. Safe-house, I thought as I eyed the crumbly face in the mirror. Who was I kidding; I should take what I can get.

The door flung open and she strutted in clacking the cheap pumps deliberately on the tile floor. She flicked her hair, pouted her lips and reached under the light blue rayon dress and pulled down the stockings. I began to sweat but being a man I couldn't look away. She turned around to the porcelain urinal and started pissing like a horse from a standing position, holding up the dress with one hand and god knows what with the other while the black stockings balanced around her knees. I thought I'd seen everything but this time I was glad I didn't. I exited before the end of what seemed like the longest piss in history and looked for a smoky booth in the corner to hide.

Needless to say she found me and I felt a bony hand on my shoulder. I didn't look around, pretended it was a spider and brushed it off.

"You playin hard to get?" she said, miffed.

"Hum a few bars and I'll see if I know it." She sat opposite me and I had to say, "There's a ladies toilet over there, do you qualify?"

"Sure, it's just too crowded in the ladies."

"Who taught you to piss like that?"

"I was raised by my dad and four brothers."

"What happened to your mother?"

"Nothin, gonna buy me a drink?"

"This doesn't mean anything, it's just a drink."

"Ok, whatever you say big boy."

She was getting overly flirty now even though I was on the pudgy side there was no need to rub it in. I ordered top shelf and she sculled it lookin for more. I nodded at the barman to bring the bottle; he was a cranky bastard and as he filled us again he looked at her and then at me and said,

"No soliciting in here sweetheart," he said, his gravelly voice threatening both of us.

"I'm not a solicitor," she said looking him up and down. He looked at me and then at the piano and I realised he wanted me to play for the sad punters strewn laconically through his sleazy lounge bar.

She looked at me and raised her eyebrows as if I had a decision to make; it was the piano or her. I looked at the piano realising it didn't want anything from me but would sit silently and wait til the next time I opened her lid and tinkled her ivories. I looked back at Blue eye shadow whose brow was now knit with expectation and even worse she was tapping her scrawny fingers on the table and waving her shoes at me. Her lipstick was starting to wear off and absorb into her thin lips. Then I remembered the bathroom incident. No contest, my eighty-eight key Kawai wasn't gonna share any disease with me other than arthritis and a bit of melancholy. Blue eyes looked like she was carrying a lot of baggage and I didn't want to compliment her cargo by being her hand held luggage.

"I hope you find what you're looking for Blue Eyes but I gotta sing for my supper."

Her shoulders slumped slightly as I slid from the smoky booth and lit another cigar. I knew she felt a little deflated but as I settled at the piano for another set, I realized she had already replaced me with an equally wretched looking wraith and they were laughing.

The barman attempted one of his smiles at me and filled my whiskey. Funny thing is, I don't inhale the smoke from the cigars and I don't drink whiskey but he paid me to look like I did. I play into the night with an Al Green song, 'Let's Stay together'.

A small school of stunned mullet shearing through the slush to the shore

Six whistling kites hovering above the flotsam of high tide

Ex-politician has coffee with two Schnauzers wearing diamante collars

Tartan hat atop Mrs Bucket and two smiling dudes in a Kombi

Ginger sets tables as sandals jog awkwardly oriental

Rays of sun pierce the grey bubbles of cloud like golden swords challenging the sea to a morning duel

Coffee comforts the early morning dip

GOLDY 2

Golden Eyes and Chuck

She was taller than me by at least eight inches including the cowgirl boots and my eyes rested comfortably on her deliberately displayed impressive cleavage recently purchased in Beverly Hills courtesy of her ex- record producer boyfriend; but that's because I was sitting at the piano.

She told me this as if I was one of her trustworthy friends ignoring the fact I was in the middle of my favourite Thelonius Monk tune. As my hands stretched out to the last bar of a rather poignant Ab13 chord progression I cast my eyes up through my rakish fringe to see if there was any other feature in her face that may be worth resting my eyes on between songs.

There they were, eyes like a Persian Panther recently escaped from the clutches of a cruel captor. They weren't any colour I had seen before, mustard, green, hazel and gold all at the same time as she flashed them around the room looking for the next kill. The fact she didn't look at me meant I was the safe haven, no threat; she knew musicians like the back of her long slender hand which was meticulously decorated with cherry red nails. I played the first notes of 'Jersey Girl' thinking she might know it and it might relax her feline twitching long enough to order a drink. She did; a margarita really salty with real lemon juice. Her curly pink lips didn't even flinch at the first desperate gulp and as she turned to talk to me I pretended I was focussed on the keyboard but I felt her knowing look through the side of my face. It was a hot appreciative look and then I caught a peripheral glimpse of her broadening, sneery smile and knew I was in trouble.

She'd spent a lot of time to make those eyebrows the right

colour and shape to frame her beguiling peepers; the whole package was designed for one thing and one thing alone.

I was pretty sure it wasn't a poor piano player with a smart mouth. Maybe I was wrong; she laid a fifty on the laminated ebony and spoke as I faltered in the middle of a key change from G to G#.

"Do you play any Doors?" she asked, knowing it was anathema to my usual jazz-funked repertoire.

"Only if they're tuned to A flat," I said without looking up.

"C'mon, everyone knows 'Love me Two Times' Chuck." Her voice was seductive and suddenly I had a nickname and possibly $50.

"I bet everyone's' loved you two times Golden Eyes". I finished 'Jersey Girl' with a distinctly Ray Manzarek feel and fled to the Gents without looking back.

The crumbling face in the mirror in front of me required a splash of cold water which never seemed to make a difference but always made me feel better looking. The door was kicked open by a well-made intricately designed line dancing boot. She was tall even when I was standing up. The longest legs I'd seen in any lavatory strutted slowly through the doorway. She turned and spread her legs into a perfect A-frame and stared me down. I was leaning back against the sink pretending, nonchalantly, that this happened to me every night but in fact my heart was racing.

She reached into her back pocket as I soaked in her steely gaze and was mesmerised by the seemingly playful allure now testing my mettle. She pulled out another fifty and said,

"Do you know the Sugar man?" I knew what she meant but said,

"Yep, he's a diabetic but I've never met Rodriguez." She wasn't impressed.

"Not the song! The Man! The Sugar man!" She waived the fifty at me again and her voice suddenly turned desperate.

"You sure you don't mean a sugar daddy sugar?"

There was a glare as her eyes darkened to a caramel disdain. Her long denimed legs were moving imperceptibly wider as the leather heels slid across the pissy tiled floor. She waited, I relinquished and looked down at my cheap fake leather shoes and said,

"See the barman, sugar, he'll sweeten you up."

A smile escaped her ridiculously curly lips and I loved her all over again. There was less quivering in her legs and she bounced her ample bosom out the door flicking the fifty with her other hand.

I followed out of morbid curiosity and was mesmerised by the rhythmic dance of her suddenly rambunctious stride towards the bar. She cut a fine figure for sure and some unlucky guy would eventually discover the cost buried beneath her treasures. The Kawai called and I answered with an extemporised version of 'Riders on the Storm' while Golden Eyes drooled knowingly at the grumpy barman who directed her to a seedy looking well-dressed man near the telephone.

The regular crowd seemed not to notice my change of genre because I gave it the same laconic jazz feel I usually apply to all my tunes which makes it sad and easy to drink to in the darkness.

Eventually she nestled herself comfortably on the Kawai feeling the vibrations in her bones, eyes glassy and distant. She tapped out the slow beat of the final fading storm of the Door's song.

Sadly, I knew her beauty would be consumed all too soon with the same melancholy affliction as our favourite self-destructive peoples' poet Mr Morrison. In the meantime, she would pause between the frantic gold-digging and contemplate the maintenance of her indestructible youth; well at least while she has me as her anchor to reality. The tragic feeding from the more tragic; just for her, I played it again.

Overly keen sun smashing into our faces

Smooth silver-green swells playing tag with each other

Tiny tot appears to glide on water, all applaud

Mullet heads bob in the south today

Grannies dancing to the waves with their inner child beaming

Sky garishly flashes its confident grin over all

Rescued baby turtle will navigate to Chile eventually

A tiny moulted feather spins to the ground from above

Headland surrounded by light and water

Another day begins

GOLDY 3

Angel

There she was clad in all her fine arrangement of purple eclectic designer clothes. I thought she looked stumpy even with the cheap fuck-me-boots half way up her pool table calves. She was cute; curly brunette with deep, burning black eyes and the sweetest black-lipped smile colour coded with the permanent black eye liner. As usual she made a B line for me as I was fingering a sexy F major 7th.

I didn't want to look at her in case I fell in love for the first time, again. I was a sucker for a sweet pucker and she was stacked so well I sensed the danger and pretended to retreat into my melancholy melody. Her voice was honey and my knees imploded, suddenly rendering me useless on the sustain pedal.

"Hi, I'm Angel. What's happening handsome?"

I just kept singing but sang at her, " Ain't no Sunshine when she's gone and she's always gone too long, anytime, she goes away.."

Then she sang the chorus in a throaty growl that numbed my conscious thought into jelly...

"I know, I know, I know, I know, I know, I know, I know, I know, I know...I oughta leave piano guy alone, cos there's no music when he's gone..."

She was good; better than I'd heard in the last drunken attempts across the piano for weeks. I played it out as she smiled knowingly at me and licked her lips. What did that mean? My man brain was on holidays in Tasmania. Was she thirsty? She was gorgeous and to my detriment she looked straight through my soul and out the back of my head. For a brief moment I was star struck and mentally slapped myself in the face and turned to smile a goofy schoolboy smile at her but she wasn't looking. Cranky Al, the barman, was cutting my grass and gladly overcharging my Angel for a double 'Sidecar' no ice.

I tried to catch her eye but she turned her back on me and sipped her lethal poison like it was milk. Still smitten like a drooling dog I watched her walk away and Al motioned me to play something. Oh yeh! I needed something to catch her attention and thought of sixty soppy love songs at once as I began to finger the keyboard trying to pick something different. 'I've been waiting for a girl like you'? or 'Girl', 'Angel Eyes', 'Send Me an Angel?" All pathetic!!

Then it came to me, 'Into my Arms', Nick Cave. I played and tried to keep the baritone voice in G. She didn't look up and callously went back to a jealousy-inducing shallow conversation with Al who was now beaming his best version of real excitement since he got five numbers in the lotto. He actually looked more like H.G. Nelson at five o'clock in the morning. The line in the song was coming up and I raised my voice just a little louder to cover the idle chatter from the booths.

"I don't believe in the existence of Angels, but lookin at you I wonder if that's true."

I looked for her reaction and she smiled wide at Al but didn't turn her head. She was playin hard to get and Al was trying to give her his phone number. I was deflated when no one applauded and walked slowly into the men's room swearing under my breath.

The mirror didn't lie and my dismal frown was smeared all over it in self-pity. I splashed my face in the hope that I would magically appear to be slightly groomed. It didn't work; I came up looking like the love child of Gary Busey and Gilda Radner, only older.

My eyes cleared and I saw a silhouette behind me and turned to see Angel staring me down like a cat playing with a leather canary. I was the canary.

"You gonna play something I like sweety?"

"What key is it in?"

"I think it starts in A flat and ends up finishing in an F.

I was a schoolboy again, averting my eyes, smiling goofily and shuffling my cheap shoes across the recently urine smeared tiles.

"Ok, what do you like?" I finally looked straight into her eyes and wished I hadn't.

"I like to start slow and build in intensity to an ear splashing climax." I shuddered. Instantly I thought of Ravel, Bolero...

"I think I've got it..." She smiled and walked me arm in arm back to the piano where I nervously tried to recreate the wind instrument at the beginning but kept realising there was already a horn in my pants so I went with a flugelhorn.

As I attempted the melody with my right hand and thrumming drums with my left I knew I was committed to 11 minutes of trying to impress Angel. My flugelhorn soon became a flute and then an oboe and I couldn't remember which wind instrument came next but she was watching me and smiling so I went straight to the discordant horn section and full orchestra climax and as I worked up a sweat I realised it was prematurely seven minutes short and the last few chords were tired and strained. Breathing heavily, I spun around to where Angel was supposed to be standing appreciatively but I only saw Al's face melting into his hands looking wistfully at the doors as Angel's sweet arse disappeared into the night. My fingers went flaccid and I watched the swinging doors til they stopped swaying.

The only woman I really wanted to get to know better than any of the others wasn't interested. My breath spilled out over the keys of the Kawai and Al noticed my face age ten years in a second. I pushed the sweat from my brow through my oily hair and looked at Al. He was still staring at the doors hoping Angel would reappear. Then he said, "Play 'Send Me An Angel'."

"Tonight Al, I drink whiskey; obviously my harp wasn't

tuned to her heart strings. Top shelf Al and I'm all yours; sing along if you know the chorus."He turned to the Glenfiddich bottle and waved my comment away in true gypsy style.

Silhouettes of pine and pandanus glow in the early
golden radiance emanating from the east

Welcoming waves giggle to the shore

Tattooed teenager tames a finless board and diamond droplets
bead on tanned skin

We skate like busy insects across the shimmering water

Left and right, gliding, paddling, chatting, whooping and smiling

Coffee waits in the crowded courtyard

Still dripping with salt, sand between the toes,
we share tall tales by the shore

Another day begins

WALK THE WALK

She walks like a tree swaying in the wind, moving with the contours of the ground, she's not in a hurry and she doesn't lead or follow. She meanders, changing her speed, occasionally kicking at things on the ground; her head down but a smile visible through her hair which hides her eyes. She doesn't care where she's going, she's just walking for the hell of it, she likes to move even if it is raining, she walks through puddles, not talking, sometimes a song escapes her lips but the words are indistinguishable, just a melody. I don't know how long we've been walking or where we are but suddenly the beach appears and the sea breeze blows her hair from her face and I see her profile, she's smiling and so are her eyes. We walk on the sand and I walk behind looking at her slender footprints, I don't want to step on them but I become transfixed as each one emerges behind her leaving a haphazard trail which is sometimes washed away by a bubbling white wave. Then the footprints stop as we hit the rocks, she gingerly picks her way through the maze of footpads and then staggers backwards to regain her balance, a little leap to get to the next granite step and a giggle at the fun of the game; we go sideways and backwards and avoid the barnacles and our arms rise up to keep our balance and then we are in the park on soft cool grass, the dewy rain has washed the sand off and we hit a boardwalk and some concrete and then dirt and it sticks to our feet. We're not even thinking of turning for home, I will follow until sunrise without tiring and then we will turn and walk back again. There is no need for talk and we don't need to be anywhere except where we are going; at this point, nothing else matters; Does it?

I notice the casual way she lets things unfold as if it is already scripted, accepting the advances of people and dogs and birds equally. Her interest focussed on what is in front of her whether other people may deem it good or bad, she has no judgement as she is part of them in this moment, in this world at the same time in this particular place. There will never be another day like it and yet she will accept all days as she does this one, with pure and genuine humanity.

It's cooling down considerably as we walk south and the winter sun is hurrying to its' western bed. The chill wind picks up our hair and threatens to steal the moisture out of our skin, whistling icy warnings past our ears; we walk faster and she shivers, closing her arms around her shoulders but still smiling with the thrill of the advent of winter. She looks at me briefly and steers her watery feet towards starboard to link up with me with her arm now firmly clinging to my arm and we fall into stride and walk into the wind like penguins to the warmth of the rookery (or like a penguin trying to steal the warmth from a husky). We've no shoes on and the asphalt is harsh and cold on her delicate feet, then she steers our ship left to the softer grass and we pad across on our toes avoiding as much contact with the cool grass as possible; ears tingling, nose reddening to counteract the Antarctic winds racing up through South Eastern Australia on this fourth day of winter. The wind is howling as leaves and dust from the roof waft into the pool forming a gyre of natural flotsam swept into one corner of the pool with each gust.

It's getting dark now as she scoops out the last remnants of jetsam from the pool, shivers audibly and tip-toes back to warmer spaces. She playfully runs the backs of her cold hands across my neck and I relish it, jump then smile back. "Let's walk," she says with a genuine fire in her eyes. With a change of clothes and comfortable shoes tied on we emerge from our cosy cocoon and suddenly start to walk up a steep rise into the starry southern twilight sky. Warm breath floating in front of our mouths, we find a rhythm and looking for a higher incline we stride towards the peak where can be seen the last rays of the sun outlining the unusually shaped volcanic cores fifty miles to the west.

Burnt orange and bruised pinks slough into the sky above us and become defiant fuchsia against the growing darkness of greys and cobalts.

We watch silently as the darkness imperceptibly creeps in from the east where the sun has no power now. Lights like fairy villages have already begun to appear below us as the automatic solar panels begin to play their part in lighting the universe; but it is in vain against the onslaught of the Milky Way constellations that have stolen the show above. Suddenly the earth is dark and has no relevance and the sky is lit with the memories of the past and the portents of the future. We gaze in neck-krinking wonder at its beauty but still with no better understanding than the inhabitants of this planet thirteen thousand years ago. The village lights flash in whites and yellows through the cool air signalling the evening settling into the comfortable routines of life; but we walk on into the night, towards the mountains.

Purposefully and without the need for nervous conversation, we march on into the cool night air noticing the change of scenery from the village lights into the much darker and unlit parts of the road west. Five miles from the village and we turn south west to follow a trail through the forest. Exposed cheeks feel the cool moist air as our breath streams out in front of us. Eyes adjust and we are in another world. Uncanny silence breathes through the trees, our footfalls finding fragile leaves crackling below but absorbed by the darkness. Suddenly the path in front of us lights up like the moon on the sea navigating us deeper into the forest. Small rustlings in the undergrowth, birds or night marsupials are hustling the ground for a meal of crawly critters. They see well in the night and flee or freeze so that you may not see them. Squawks from the trees ahead alert us to the presence of flying fox chittering and squealing away at each other sensing our closeness with radar precision but we pose no threat and continue along the illuminated path. We sense each other's breathing but do not speak as the rhythm of our strides is purposeful and relaxed.

The trees thin, revealing a glade lit up by the rising moon and we stop to take in the scene, eyes adjusting again after the dark forest. "What's that?" she asks, pointing to the far side of the clearing.

A shadow senses our presence and slinks back into the darker shadows behind it, turning suddenly to see if we follow and the red reflections of the moonlight leave us in no doubt that it is a fox. Briefly, there is a distinctive scent and then it is gone. We stand in the silence listening.

To our left at the bottom of a gradual slope comes the high pitched tinkle of water over rocks. We walk gingerly, testing the ground in the pale light and eventually stand at the edge of a small waterfall. Again, it needs no comment; no human utterings will make it better than it is. There is no passing of time measured by the steady flow of moonlit water over rocks. Our spell is broken by an owl's soft double hoot; Boobook; his eyes turn to us but are yellow, wide and unafraid. It turns, disappears on silent wings and we hear no more than a whisper. We follow the water slowly downstream along the bank. Stepping stone rocks appear, crossing the stream. We step into the middle looking into the increasing darkness of the creek bed, listening to the water disappear into deeper eddies. The unexplored side of the creek beckons us cautiously as it rises up to what appear to be shadows against the sky. High pillars looming into the night like guardians of some ancient fortress. We climb, not looking back and push on through whichever paths we find and re-find to get us to the pillars. Our breath now fluming in front of us as we reach cooler altitudes; we slow and muscles burning, we enter a thin forest of gums either side of a trail which hugs the edge of the escarpment. It appears to be rising gradually like that left by a cow who will always find the path of least resistance. Now we can see down into the valley as we walk. The creek sparkles below like a thread of silver winding between huge thickets of bush; disappearing only to re-appear briefly, hide again.

The trail is taking us around the back of the huge pillars as we start to wind left in a spiral towards the top. There are some boulders to squeeze between and some to scale.

The trail appears to stop and we pause again to look down into the now deeper valley with its sharp inclines and precariously positioned boulders. "There it is," I say, seeing the path on the other side of a lump of granite. We continue to wind left up the hill and the pillars come into sight but they look completely different now that we are behind them. The silhouettes resemble a tribe of people walking north in single file towards the emerging dragons-eye moon. Slowly we approach them; eventually standing between two massive towers composed of red and grey conglomerate rock pushed up from the creek bed many millennia past. The wind howls up the ridge between the ancient guards and blows our hair around in a mini cyclone.

The village shimmers to the east in the distance like a hive of fireflies buzzing around a queen. Stars form a dragon around the yellowing eye of the moon. Again the wind gusts through myriad cracks and holes in the rocks, whispering its intent as it has done endlessly since the dream time. The voices of the tribe are singing as they walk from place to place. There is another path to the right of the pillars and we pick our way carefully along the edge to hide from the relentless assault of the wind. The distant whispering recedes as we follow the straight gradual path down; not a cow trail this time but the path made by water running off the hill. It is gravelly and loose and we begin to slide then quickly sit down to slow the ride. We do this six or seven times before stumbling the last steep bit into another cool forest. Dusted off and assured of healthy limbs we look around and listen. Our presence was probably heard all the way down the slope and everything in the forest had hidden or gone into freeze mode.

The wind above is now hardly noticeable. We follow the water course through the trees until it forks into three around the further side of a massive fir pine. We are drawn to it and sense its presence compared to the rest of the forest. The scaly grey bark is cool and gives off a slight hint of pine tree perspiration.

The branches above us sway gently seeming to point the way through the forest. Our eyes meet briefly and without a word we nod and walk along the middle trail of the three forks.

"It smells good in here," I say under my breath, lifting my nose into the air.

"Mmmm, night jasmine," she says smiling and striding boldly into the cool darkness.

We follow the sweetness as many generations before had done without the need of satnav; instinct drew us forward, confident, excited at the prospect of new and wonderful discoveries. We felt no weariness, no pain from the constant walking; no thirst, no hunger, no fear. It smells good in here. And it did… eucalypts, callistemon, Banksia, honeysuckle, wattle, and grevilleas. But there were other olfactory nuances in the rising petrichor amongst the decomposing leaves and deadwood. The distinctive arresting pungency of mould in its various forms feeding on rotting timbers.

The 'scent of the bush' wafting elusively and briefly as you try to chase it down with a turn of the head. We are still walking along the middle trail but it widens suddenly into an avenue of uniform geometric lines of the same type of tree, each one a replica of the other. They disappear into the distance like a clever Escher engraving. Each way you look, you see the same linear patterns which could only have been designed by mathematics rather than nature. We pause, allowing the moon to appear from behind a rogue cloud so we can view the spectacle of soldiers marching in all directions at the same time and yet motionless. Only our movement and perspective can give them movement. We walk faster and realise that our speed forwards has made the soldiers appear to march in our peripheral vision.

But only we knew, according to the moon and stars that we were heading south; the soldiers did not appear to know which direction they should be advancing and to us they appeared to be going in all directions at the same time. Suddenly, we slow, simultaneously sensing movement to our left and then stop to listen. The soldiers stop with us and stand to silent attention. Nothing; wind through the tops of the trees, then a rustle in the bed of needles beneath one of the soldiers. We freeze, look, listen; keeping eye contact through a perspicacious brow. Movement around our feet and the moonlight reflects the snake scales with alarming clarity. We do not panic, watching with curiosity rather than fear as we are blessed with the welcoming committee whose ancestors date well beyond most other creatures on the planet. Mutual respect as the serpent slithers into the silence behind us looking for an easier supper to digest. Minutes pass in silence before we smile and move on, but this time in a different direction. The soldiers give us a guard of honour as we head west away from the chasing moon; ears still pricked for any other slithery commotion. Shoes on the pine needles soon give way to noisy gravel and dirt. The road goes south to north but we cross straight over and continue west. She turns and smiles at me and I respond equally, sharing her excitement at what may lay ahead. Large cleared fields open up beyond a barbed wire fence which we duck through and enter amongst a herd of Brahman feeding placidly in the moonlight. They give no more than a glance our way as we do not smell like fox or dog, but like the creature which feeds and protects them.

Careful not to disturb the dung beetle ridden pats of warm four-stomach digested grass, we tip-toe between the two ton beasts silently and they indiscriminately nod their heads to allow us passage through their world. It smells good by the way. The wind has faded quickly leaving an eerie silence highlighted by the rising moon and the shadows it projects through the gum trees. Sounds of munching molars are now audible as we stop briefly to listen to nocturnal bovine rumination. It's highly recommended on our list of 'must do' things in this area.

The field is lit by the pale dragon's eye moon. To our right near the creek, tiny fireflies flash their blue neon tails at us and dance around each other as though we had disturbed their annual ball. We smell the cool moisture rising from the creek and again hear the trickle of water falling. We tiptoe across on four similar sized rocks. Something is moving noisily through the bush and we freeze to listen. Briefly we see the flash of red in the eyes of three fast moving dogs. Without hesitation we climb the nearest tree on the creek bed and sit silently waiting for them to pick up our scent. Soon enough they pause and head straight for the base of the tree sniffing the ground and then looking up at the branches to see us sitting silently.

One is as big as a Great Dane with black and white spots, another is darker and more like a Rottweiler, the third is smaller and looks to have been crossed with a stag hound with its wiry tan coat and facial hair. They growl and bark trying to climb the tree by standing on their hind legs pressing their forepaws on the trunk but can go no further. Our adrenalin and slight fear seems to have been detected by them and they continue to circle looking to intimidate an easy prey but we sit silent and still. I whisper something to her and she counts, 1, 2, 3 then we yell with all our might into the night until our voices croak with lack of breath.

The dogs momentarily move away defensively and we repeat the yell three times at them until they decide to retreat but we wait for thirty minutes before being satisfied that they have moved on.

Once on the ground and listening hard for signs of canine activity we choose some sturdy hardwood sticks as defensive weapons and jog up the creek to avoid being detected. I also lodge some choice smooth rocks from the creek into my pockets, just in case.

We are on high alert as we approach a barbed wire fence crossing the creek. We can easily duck under it but cattle would have much more trouble negotiating the rocks and the wires.

The creek suddenly disappears underground and we emerge into a small clearing surrounded by massive Bunya pines. In the centre we see white shapes reflecting the moonlight which, on closer inspection, turns out to be the bones of dead cattle. This is the place they come to die when they are old. Dozens of skulls and ribs and giant femurs in different levels of decomposition, some moved or ravaged by the wild dogs and other carnivorous creatures. We stare in reverence for a minute or so still listening carefully for the wild dogs.

From the ridge up on the right we hear human sounds; yelling and whistling perhaps someone calling in their dogs. Could it be they weren't wild after all but farm dogs let loose for the night? Surely no farmer would allow his working dogs to run wild. What if they come back this way?

We move faster up the creek back to higher ground and see a light coming from a house perched on the ridge to the left among the trees and are instinctively drawn towards it; a safe haven if the dogs find us.

We skirt the property without trespassing and suddenly find a dirt road heading east and downhill. The feint scent of a wild guava tree assaults our senses and we follow the smell until we are standing under it. We pick some fruit and tear open the flesh sucking out the tangy pink treat and spit the seeds where we are standing. We hadn't realised how hungry we were til right then but avoid having too many so as not to upset our relatively empty stomachs with too much acid. I wipe the juice from my mouth with the back of my forearm and hand. She does the same.

Relieved to be away from the dogs, we laugh at how close we came to being mauled and I dump most of my rocks near the road but we keep the sturdy branches as walking sticks and maybe still protection. Not sure where it leads, we follow the road down and see more lights in the distance. We have no concept of time at this point in this strange place. She walks close to me, holds my arm to pause me and kisses me gently on the lips. As she pulls away I pull her back and kiss her again for twice as long. The moon suddenly clouds over as a light shower begins to fall around us. It lasts a few seconds.

Unperturbed, we walk on embracing the coolness of the mist on our faces. With sticks in unison on the dirt road we continue to walk the walk.

We are in each other's moment striding downhill in time to an unheard rhythm. Distant lights from farmhouses silhouette their occupants moving around inside and the smells of their nightly dinner waft towards us. We guess what they are having based on the smells alone. There is definitely steak cooking somewhere. The sweet aroma of a pie baking enters our nostrils and we look at each other smiling. The road leads down to an intersection and we look right then left. The rain intensifies and we look for shelter. A large mango tree nearby provides some protection but we huddle together for warmth and press against the trunk to minimise being soaked by the water dripping from the leaves.

Occasionally we stand under a drip and open our mouths to slake a previously unrecognised thirst. She is not perturbed at all by our situation, standing in the night waiting for the shower to pass. She shivers excitedly and her face glows with what can only be a childish expression of fun. The rain lessens, the drips slow and we step out onto another dirt road heading south-west and up a steep slope.

The rain has made it slippery and muddy in places but we plough on regardless not knowing where it will lead. The lights of a car flash around the corner in front of us and come roaring down the hill. We step off the road and stand perfectly still beside a lantana bush. The car slides carelessly near us on the mushy road throwing mud and water in our direction but the driver is oblivious to our presence in the shadows. We watch the red tail lights fishtail recklessly round the next corner before we continue. A boobook hoots above us from a bottlebrush tree seeming to admonish the inconsiderate driver.

Up and up we walk as the road gets steeper. Our breathing labours and we walk half bent over using our sticks for support, the other hand on a knee as our progress slows. We pause momentarily and turn around to look at how high we have climbed. Our wet clothes have now mingled with the sweat of exertion and cling uncomfortably.

I remove my shirt and tuck it into the back elastic of my shorts. The air is cooling on my skin. I run my fingers through my hair to push it back from my face and breathe deeply.

She removes a layer of clothing and ties it round her waist. We look at each other, smiling in disbelief at where we are and perhaps at the stupidity of what we are doing but there is no going back. We continue to walk the walk. How long can we go for? When will we decide to turn for home? The excitement of the walk has put aside any thoughts of exhaustion or hunger and we continue as though we are pre-programmmed to arrive at an unknown destination; driven onwards by some mystical compass. After some time we crest the top of the hill and stand at the crossroads.

Is there a right way to go or do we follow our instincts? The answer comes from the sweet scent of a lily-pilly to our right. She moves towards the aroma like a bee to a rose and begins to pick the fuchsia coloured berries. We stand in the crossroads looking south at the twinkling yellow lights of the civilization we have left behind. The berries are sweet and sour at the same time as we nibble them carefully, spitting the seeds under the tree from which they sprouted. A dog barks wildly in the distance, waking us from our musing of the landscape far below. We look at each other and move off quietly tightening our grip on the hardwood walking sticks.

"Wait!" she says and I pause. She reaches down to my calf muscle and rips a leech from it as though it were a band aid. She holds it in front of my face then spins me around to look for more. Another one further up my leg and it is engorged with my blood.

This time it hurts and I wince and see the blood flowing freely down my leg. Confident she has found no more, she demands, "Check me!"

In the dim moonlight, I twirl her around and mostly through feel rather than sight find none; "Wait, what's that?" I ask feeling carefully around her waist. "It's a mole" she says quietly. I check again and look carefully at her shapely legs now glistening from the sweat of walking up the hill. Just above her sock I feel the unmistakable shape of a cattle tick. "Hold still," I say and she cranes around trying to see what it is. Using my fingernails to firmly grasp the head, I push it in and twist it violently anti-clockwise and pull.

"Ow! What is it?" I show her the small crusty parasite and she smiles, amused at our mutual blood-letting. I check her again and she checks me before we are satisfied there is nothing else attached to our bodies without our permission. We embrace, appreciating the importance of having close contact with each other, for without each other, we may falter.

We are walking east without purpose or map or destination in mind when we see the pale dawn emerging over the eastern horizon. We have been walking since late afternoon the previous day with a short stop at home to change clothes. Following the landscape rather than the road, we walk directly towards the eastern light. Through fields and wilderness, noticing the orange and purple dawn chasing away the starlit night behind us, we tramp rhythmically not speaking but with a shared song in our heads.

She hums something inaudible and I recognise that it is a happy song. I begin to whistle the same tune; she stops and puts a hand on my bare chest and smiles. There is nothing better in my life than that moment when her eyes meet mine. A connection, recognition, shared thought in the darkest part of the night just before sunrise. She sees a wild raspberry bush and runs towards it. The berries have been freshly washed by the rain and are sweet.

I join the foraging between 'mmmm' sounds emanating from deep within her throat. She crushes the berries between her teeth and the juice bleeds out onto her lips. She licks the juice up with a swift tongue, pushes one into my mouth and I relish the experience, realising I haven't eaten for nearly twenty four hours, apart from the wild guavas and lily-pillies, but I am sated by the generosity of her intentions to give me sustenance so we may continue our mystical journey. I do not thirst and I need nothing beyond this moment. We continue to walk the walk as the sunrise peeps over the horizon and temporarily blinds us with its pure light.

We pause and see the outlines of mountains revealed by the sun's rays. I know where we are now. I know the landscape; I know the way home. I put my now dry shirt back on and lead us to the northeast. We have to skip across highways amidst early morning traffic and are confronted with tall, strayed sugar cane stalks and ditches with the previous nights' rain sitting in the hollows by the road. The humidity is increasing with every step eastwards so we traverse around the hills to avoid exertion. The rising sun still dictates our direction. We follow the river and its riparian fringe, suddenly being accosted by mosquitoes and midges which haven't filled their nightly quota. I spot a ti-tree and rub the bark and leaves on our arms. I wave a branch around us as we walk, repelling most of the blood sucking, vampiric insects but we are mottled with different bites as we emerge into the clearing of the flatlands leading to the sea. The blood on our legs has coagulated into scabs.

Suddenly, the sun peeks over the horizon like the 'Eye of Sauron' highlighting us in the landscape. Instantly, the air becomes cool and we stride towards the east with a purpose. The land is flat beside the river after the sugar cane harvest. The sound of toads, frogs, crickets and water pea hens surround us. We tread carefully in case we wake a slumbering snake.

The river meanders before us to the sea. To the right, a creek bed branches off towards the south-east, our ultimate destination only fourteen miles beyond. We follow the creek.

The rotting and muddy scent of mangroves greets us but we follow it unquestioningly. The vegetation thickens and we realise we will have to make our own path through the wilderness. We still have our walking sticks and I wave the ti-tree branch to ward off the native phlebotomists. The smell of honey stops us. Our noses rise into the air trying to track the source. Of course, the soft floral bouquets of the melaleucas appear nearby. We run our hands through the flowers and sniff deeply at the subtle scent. Native bees lead us to the sweet hive and we dip our fingers fearlessly into the sugarbag. Licking our fingers clean of the sweet dark honey, we dip again with no resistance from the bees. We move on without disturbing the pristine environment, walking with renewed purpose. Kangaroos and wallabies hop away from us in all directions.

The humidity increases markedly and we begin to sweat. Our shoes and socks are still soaked and they slosh with every step. The river to our left attracts us. At the bank of the river we see a sandy trail, remove our shoes and tie them around our necks by the laces. We follow the sandy edge barefoot as it emerges into the mouth of the river. The feint susurration of the surf blows intermittently from the east and we smell the salty sea ahead. It urges us on and the cooling breeze greets our sweaty bodies. We sigh in appreciation. The surf grows louder and unexpectedly a cloud covers the sun relieving the humidity. Once again, I am following her shapely footprints in the sand stepping into each one trying to imitate her stride. She turns to me smiling and dances backwards up the deserted beach. I playfully try to step into her footsteps as she skips left and right. I feel truly free and emotionally wealthier than anyone on the planet at this time.

We embrace for what seems like an eternity and then turn and walk hand in hand to the south. The cloud slides away from the sun and we are bathed in bright light again.

Home is still far away but we walk the walk with no thought of danger or anxiety; no judgement, no expectations. We are in the moment, appreciating the changing landscape, the fluffy clouds over the ocean and the ships way out to sea. Gulls mill about near the shoreline looking for an easy breakfast before people invade their pristine world. A whistling kite hovers above us adjusting its wings perfectly to the light breeze. Hundred year old pine trees line the shore ahead of us belying the existence of ancient invaders from a northern land. Flocks of colourful, noisy lorikeets swoop past us on their way to the flowering callistemon and honeysuckles.

An early morning surfer stands on the beach contemplating the best banks to surf. He looks in our direction and waves before he plunges into the cool green sea, paddling through the break, duck diving like a penguin.

We reach the headland and begin to negotiate the rocks around the edge of the cliff. We play a game called 'don't touch the sand' leaping from stone to stone balancing and backtracking and intuitively choosing the next footfall. She leads; I follow onto each randomly chosen rock, some of which are slippery. With our hands raised in the air for balance and shoes precariously swinging around our necks we make it past the headland to the next stretch of beach. The sand disappears into the distance like a mirage covered with salt spray.

We walk silently across the undulating dunes created by the previous night's tide noticing the flotsam and jetsam washed up on the high tide mark. Occasionally we pause to pick up an oddity and share it with each other; a zebra shark egg, tiny oyster shells, soft orange coral and mangrove seeds. We see tiny plastics and collect them into our pockets without a word being exchanged.

After some time, our feet are beginning to be abrazed by the constant footsteps on the sand. We pause and replace our shoes and socks to avoid any permanent damage to the now sensitive skin on our feet. The sun has risen higher and I tear off my shirt again as she untucks her cotton top from her cotton shorts and unbuttons it to allow the sea breeze onto her skin. We forge on feeling a building thirst in the heat of the mid-morning sun.

A freshwater creek ahead of us flows into the ocean with its tea-tree stained brown water making tiny random patterns in the sand. She walks further up the dune to the source and carefully sips the water. I copy her movements, appreciating the cool sweetness of the ancient filtered water and we turn for the last leg of our walk.

No time seems to have passed as we approach our home beach and begin to walk up the road to our house. The familiar landscape is comforting and re-assuring. The house is as we left it; quiet and unpretentious. Once inside we walk into the cool pool fully clothed and float, remembering the images and landscape we had traversed in the last twenty four hours. We peel off our clothes and shoes and embrace. She says, "Let's do it again tomorrow."

GOLDY 4

Flames

She strode in like a mythical creature, her long giraffe like legs managing to direct her white stilettos in a fluid strut across the sticky carpet. Her head was aflame, no, I mean fully alight with curls flowing out from every direction somewhere between Carol Lloyd and the Venus on the Half Shell. It was an art piece in hairdressing that would have made Medusa envious. The little black number hanging off her coat hanger shoulders was an obvious ruse to show off her alabaster skin glowing in the stage lights and accentuating her sleek physique. She didn't look at anyone, striding elegantly towards the bar; needless to say Al was already rubbing his hands together in anticipation of making another over-priced toxic masterpiece cocktail he'd never heard of. She wasn't carrying a purse and I guessed she might have a little boob stash so I played 'Popsicle Toes'; "you've got the nicest North America, this sailor ever saw..."

"Beer," she said with a lilting dismissive tone.

"You Irish then?" asked Al glancing up at the flames dancing on her head.

"No, just thirsty," she said with a small hint of a smile on her full lips. She reached into her 38's and pulled out a fifty neatly folded and handed it to Al. He probably kept that one for posterity. She turned to look at me and then I saw them on her heart-shaped face; beautiful freckles that she obviously didn't want to cover up; a unique feature on such an exquisite creature. I made a mental note for a song.

She leaned on the bar and took in her surroundings before deciding where to light the fire. I was getting a pretty good look in when Mario the Romancing Dancer twinkle toed through the swinging doors and spotted the burning gazelle at the bar and made a B line for her as I played 'This Old Love' by Lior.

I tried to stall him by calling him over but he just waved and kept on his missile-like trajectory to the luminous legs like an overloaded ship to a lighthouse. She saw him coming and ordered another beer. Mario was a full 6 inches shorter than her but that hadn't stopped him before.

"Well hello lovely lady, would you like to dance?"

"No thank you sir, I'm not very good with these shoes and I think it would look something like a freak show."

"I can show you signorina," and he reached for her arm.

"Touch me and I'll give you an arse bleaching with this beer bottle and rip your moustache off," she said calmly.

Mario was stopped in his tracks and she glared him away. He sheepishly slumped at the end of the bar apologising to her and tried to smile sweetly at her as though he wasn't such a bad guy after all.

Al was holding back a laugh and had to turn around so as not to be seen but Flames was enjoying her beer and did not seem the least bit less graceful or perturbed by Mario's failed incursion.

To lighten up the mood I played 'Light My Fire' and directed it towards the fiery furnace at the bar. "Our love burns like a funeral pyre….. " She blew me a kiss and I shuddered and lost my sustain pedal foot into the piano and my shoe was stuck inside with my foot still in it.

I pretended not to notice and adjusted my position on the stool with an awkward twist, fudged the ending of the song and smiled goofily back at her with my foot stuck in the piano. She motioned me over with her finger and in my enthusiasm to get there fell flat on my face in the sticky carpet with my foot still stuck in the piano. Al looked over at me on the floor and then turned to Flames and said, laughing, "He doesn't even drink."

I managed to get my foot out and pushed myself up quickly

from the floor to show I was fine and in the process knocked a glass of stale piss and butts onto my new chinos at the crotch. I looked at Flames and said, "Gimme a minute" and pointed to the gents. She nodded with a wry smile and held up her beer in salute. Needless to say Mario was chuckling away with Al at the end of the bar.

The GENTS, although empty, was occupied by a foul demon of someone else's gas. I cringed and looked at the face in the mirror and wasn't shocked to see a mummified skull staring back at me with gum in my hair and someone's hair stuck to my face as a result of the sticky carpet push ups I was doing earlier. I splashed my face with water and looked at the face again trying to see who was in those empty eyes opposite me but drew a blank, again. My chinos were beyond saving and I avoided putting more liquid on them and padded them with a napkin, groomed myself with a bit of spit and launched for the door feeling fifty years younger than when I first walked in. Too late, Flames couldn't wait. She pushed the GENTS door inward and sent me sliding across the piss-stained floor on my back.

With my hands and feet in the air I watched her stride towards me and lift her long left leg onto the wall above my head. I couldn't help but look and she said, "What does that look like?"

Considering the flames now highlighted above her head I said, "A rusty map of Tassie?"

"Not that; look at my left ankle!"

I looked and sure enough there was a birth mark in the shape of a piano. Still on the floor I perched my head on my hand to get a closer look and saw that some of the freckles near it looked like musical notes.

"So, that's not a tattoo?" I asked looking up again at her sweet heart –shaped face framed in fire. Much to my dismay, she lowered her leg and I raised myself from the floor and washed my hands as she spoke. She smelled good too and I thought that at least one of us should.

"A gypsy fortune teller told me I was going to meet a talented piano player who would sweep me off my feet."

"You've already done that to me twice." I said peeling the chewing gum out of my hair and smelling my jacket.

"Play me something I can get my teeth into and I'll buy you a drink," she said now close enough I could see her freckly face and green eyes up close; ...stunning!

"What do you like?" I asked trying to stand downwind from her but keeping my face close enough to do a mental 'dot-to-dot' across her face freckles.

"I like fun music, something to dance to; do you dance?" She wiggled her hips at me and I nearly blew a head gasket as her little black number threatened to ride up her silky thighs.

"Er, not while I'm playing piano." She laughed.

"You're funny; I think that's the most redeeming quality to have. You don't take yourself too seriously." I looked in the mirror and said, "If I did I wouldn't look like this."

She laughed again; a very innocent laugh that came from way down deep inside her.

The image from the bathroom floor flashed back at me and I coughed nervously.

"So what do you do Flames?" She didn't flinch.

"I model for Sailor Jerry Rum."

"Lucky bastard, how is Jerry? He owes me money!" I said following her swaying hind quarters to the bar admiringly. Look out flugelhorn!

Al was waving his hands at me to play so I had to let her go for a while. She boothed up with another beer and sat directly opposite me on a high stool which provided me with a private viewing of lengthy thighs which only served to distract me from my playing. After two songs she walked like a prey animal to the piano and said, "Did you call me 'Flames' because of my hair Sailor honey?"

"No, it's just because you're so hot," I said beginning to play 'Hotter than July'.

She smiled wide and flipped a 'Sailor Jerry' coaster at me and slinked into the night.

All I could hope was there was a phone number on the other side.

You took my breath away, I don't know why;
I'm not usually a very sentimental kind of guy

Something about the way you moved, a bird through the air
then when your eyes met mine, your little smile;
I fell into a romantic despair

Knowing from that fleeting moment that you were the one
My mind was always with yours after the setting of each sun

I longed to hear you talk to me and look into your eyes
It took an unguarded moment to see through your disguise

You danced through the night like it was your God-given right
Smiling at this guy, I don't know why;
but we danced through the night

Here's something for you lovers of spontaneous verse
Where assonance and alliteration tend to traverse

I'm hoping for understanding, at least in a few,
that what I have written is solely for you

As magic as the petrichor smells, I shall impart a new rite
Which may set some readers on a path to being erudite

Sublime and subliminal are parts of our minds
Which are manifest in our many humanitarian kinds

From here to eternity shall the words re-ignite?
The sad decline of the technological communication blight

Data and numbers do not dictate our lives
As we kiss and hug our husbands and wives

So live in the present, express your true self
You don't want to be the one left on the shelf

Think of the future and what you will do next
Learn from the past, always do your very best

GOLDY 5

Lall

She just appeared at the piano already halfway through her own conversation.

"Names Lall, I'm 43,"she said. I thought she looked much older and countered with a complimentary, "There's no way you look 43," and played a few snippets from 'Autumn Leaves'.

"Thank you," she said, rearranging her outdated clothes across her ample chest. Her hair was mousey and unkempt and the dark rings around her generic parrot eyes were not a result of makeup.

"I've just come from my fourth fucking divorce," she squawked in her most alluring voice. At that point I knew I wanted her to shut up. She continued talking, balancing a precariously long cigarette ash over the Kawai while gesturing with her bony nail-less hands. As the ash fell I breathed out and blew it into her lap. She brushed it off and looked at the ceiling fans as the culprit and then looked back at me.

"Do you know why they left me?" she asked with a slight Ipswich accent. I felt compelled to ask.

"I can't imagine why any man would want to lose such an asset Lall." I pounded my hand on the bass keys to drown out the whiny voice but she raised her volume easily above my din as though she'd done it a thousand times before to make herself heard.

"The first one left me for a younger woman, his sister's best friend." I reached for the special tip jar on the other end of the piano and placed it in front of her dangling ash. She obliged even though the sign on the jar said, 'Psychiatric Help $5' Needless to say, it was empty except for the ash; no cash.

"The second one was a bit younger and I realised he was just going with me to get to my sister. She had bigger tits than me so I went and got these." She proudly held both of them in her hands doing an impersonation of a dead heat in a Zeppelin race.

"Very impressive," I said, "How much?" I pretended to be playing a difficult piece and mimed turning music pages and concentrating. It was a three chord Elton John song but she seemed not to notice.

"After I got these," she wheezed with perfect emphysemic punctuation, "I met my third husband and he was a fiery red-headed titty monster who took my car and ran off with the butchers' gay 19 year old son."

"Sounds like you can pick em Lall." She didn't blink, finished her Holiday Virginia fag sucking it into the filter and dumping it into my tip jar still burning. I was playing 'Hey Lord Don't Ask me Questions' by Graham Parker and the Rumour while she continued.

"But I got wise eventually and found myself an older more gentlemanly fellow called Norm who was a mining magnate. Sure, he was 70 and fat but he was loaded and had bad eyesight."

"That helps sometimes," I said finishing my song with a flurry. She continued after a slug of Bacardi and Diet Coke and motioned for Al to refill her.

"This time, I divorced after eighteen months and took what I was due. Now, I'm a fucking millionaire." She laughed an almost toothless open- mouthed cackle and reached for another cigarette from the packet of 40 sitting on the piano. Sensing an escapist opportunity I fled to the GENTS as Al placed the drink in front of her.

He'd overheard the millionaire comment and tried to strike up a conversation and procured a real ashtray for her. She looked at him as he tried to smile at her.

"Jeez, you're fuckin ugly aren't you mate," she said as

54

though Al had just been dismissed as a possible fifth husband.

"I'll take that as a compliment," he said, obviously mesmerised by the lure of easy money attached to a 40DD chest. He could put up with anything after his 7 failed attempts to make someone an honest woman.

The bathroom space held its usual stinky appeal and there was toilet paper all over the cubicles and taps. I splashed some water in my face and looked up at the penniless dishevelled piano player in the mirror. I didn't look too bad considering the face I'd been looking at for the last ten minutes. The name 'Lall' seemed to suit her considering where she'd been up to this point. Hard Yards...

The door burst open and Al appeared in a panic.

"Do you know CPR?" he said with his wide appealing hands.

"No, but I know CCR, why?"

"She's collapsed on the floor, c'mon."

"Call an ambulance Al, she can afford it," I said returning to my futile grooming in the mirror.

"And she vomited on your piano!"

Now he had my attention. I swore, thinking of poor Kawai and made for the door. Al followed.

There she was lying still and quiet but with vomit strewn across her lacquered finish and into the new strings; poor Kawai.

Then I saw the frail body with unshaved legs and networks of veins growing out of the back of her knees. She was face down and drooling onto the sticky carpet with her glass still in her hand. Al looked at me. "Well?" he asked.

"Have you called the ambos?"

"Yeh, but what do we do now?" He was panicky.

"You'll have to give her CPR," I said beginning to clean up the piano. "I'll tell you what to do."

Al got down on the floor, rolled her over and removed the glass. He could see the 40DD's reaching up to his eyeballs and then looked at me.

"Take her pulse, in the neck." He did and there was a feint beat.

"Is she breathing?"

Al leant down to listen to her mouth and was positioned centimetres above the Silicon Mountains either side of his head. He nodded 'no' and I said, "Give her two breaths and watch her chest rise."

He sort of grimaced at the thought and then wiped his mouth and blew into hers. Her chest wasn't rising.

"Take her clothes off Al and loosen the pressure around her chest."

It was getting comedic as Al fumbled for the secure clips at the back of Lall's bra. He had to straddle her body and sit her up to release the clip. The punters had all come in to see Al's burlesque show and I played a French Moulin Rouge type of run on the keyboard but Al glared at me that this was no time for jokes.

As the last clip gave under pressure, the bra flung off straight into Al's face and Lall's 40DD's sprung into life as everyone gasped audibly and stared. I played an escalating scale and plinked the high C.

Al laid her down, stood up with the bra in his hand and joined everyone in ogling what he thought was a treasure chest. The ambos ambled in and calmly assessed the situation seeing the semi-naked woman on the floor in a circle of onlookers.

"Is she breathing?" asked one.

Al, still mesmerised, replied, "I don't think so but she has a pulse." He handed the bra to the female ambo and stood back. They checked her airways and found some obstruction; just as they were about to attempt to move it she coughed, sat up, coughed again and spat out my tip jar sign, 'Psychiatric Help $5'.

I quickly picked it up and put it on the piano as everyone

gasped at her sudden recovery.

"Thanks Lall, I've been looking for that; have you met the owner Al? He saved your life."

Al sheepishly waved at her from behind the ambos and when Lall realised her semi-naked condition on the floor, began to giggle and the 40DD's giggled with her and then everyone else joined in.

Buoyed by the support of her crowd, Lall stood unsteadily, raised her hands to her breasts and said,

"What do you think of these little beauties? They saved me from hitting my head on the floor, again."

She cackled and everyone cheered, applauded and whistled and I played a Bondi Cigars song called, "You're never really drunk till you're clinging to the floor."

Al shouted the bar, the ambos stayed for a knock off drink and Lall found a potential husband number 5 while wearing her bra for the rest of the evening.

I played a medley of Elton songs including, 'I wanna kiss the bride', 'I'm still standing' and 'too low for zero'.

I'm reticent in coming forward and liberal with a smile
I don't care much for fashion so I choose a classic style

Jeans are always comfortable and cotton is a given
Wool will keep me warm at night accompanied by a mitten

My head is warm because I wear a beanie or a cap
My canine friend seems comfortable just lying in my lap

Socks and shoes are optional depending on the cold
But snuggling has benefits that are better so I'm told

When you're at home it's your domain, a place you can relax
And don't get caught up in the world of high fashion and syntax

Just before sunrise in the grey cloud cover
We sipped a small strong cup of coffee
Down the hill came a string of silent lights smashing into our faces
Like Shane McGowan's smile

Random and yet spaced safely apart from each other
Came the line of early morning alien cyclists
They turned left, right, from where we sat and then right,
right from where we sat
Heading for a coffee shop that was still a long way
From the end of the ride

A crazy diver splashed in the bay at shark feeding time
And made us pause for reflection on what he could see
In the early lightless sea
Hopefully not a man in a grey suit or the propeller of a boat
Or a giant megalodon

Pacing through the Shelley Beach forest
We wax rhapsodically about people
Joggers with ear pieces pass us from the front and rear
And don't return our greetings

Puffing back to our houses for poached eggs and bacon,
Another day begins

My walk was brief but it came with free heat
As my shoes completely stifled my feet

Just a hint of breeze now as I climb the hill
And my ankle has developed a clicky free will

There's the hope of rain just teasing the sky
And a dog on a mission, ignores me, runs by

Only two stars through the thick humid cloud
One for me, one for you, shining through a moist shroud

Then it's silent except for a ship on the sea
Blasts its foghorn to warn all the fishermen like me

As I watch from a distance the ship sails by
And I turn for home, bid the lighthouse goodbye

All downhill from here, a slight wind in my face
I count 300 steps to the door of my place

GOLDY 6

Diana and the Ram

The moment she walked into the bar everyone else was instantly punching above their weight. I wasn't even in her universe as she was wearing the pale blue of a Neptune influenced star sign and I was the mere background earth sign that framed her magnificence. Her eyes seemed to be constantly smiling even though she could only see the sad silhouettes of Al and me trying to fill the dark spaces. Her presence seemed to carry a glow which she moved fluidly to the bar. Al was almost thrown backwards by her fluorescent smile and when he saw her crystal blue eyes he froze as if it was the moment he'd waited for as the most propitious time to die.

He gurgled a greeting in Martian which she didn't need to translate and asked for champagne.

"Of course madam," Al lisped as he thought about his Costco-priced cellar of cheap Passion Pop. There was one bottle he'd purloined from his cousins' funeral that might just be suitable for such an 'other-worldly' figure as Diana. She still had her name tag on from the 'Alternative Energies' conference she was attending upstairs so Al addressed her as such and presented the gold–foiled bottle to her as a gift to a goddess.

"Does this suit Diana?" he said in his worst Sylvester Stallone impersonation.

"Yes, that's fine, thank you," she replied, her voice melding into the thick air of the bar like the coo of a white dove.

As she held her innocent court at the bar, Al looked busy trying to procure an elegant ice bucket to suit the occasion and ended up emptying a yellow aluminium 70's pot plant of its unfortunate mother-in-laws tongue and tipped as much ice as he could find around the openly displayed expensive bottle of bubbles. I thought I should play something to suit the occasion of visiting royalty and began 'God Save The Queen' but quickly changed to "Begin the Beguine'. The dance had begun. She quickly turned her face towards me and I tried to look at her like George Clooney through my seriously furrowed eyebrows without making a big deal of it but when she made eye contact and lifted her glass to me I floundered, thinking I'd somehow made a quantum leap into her universe but I deflated noticeably when I realised she was making contact with another of her kind who was standing directly behind me wearing the same coloured halo as she wore. It was the Ram; I'd seen him before. He was a modest muscle bound hunk who shared the same coloured eyes as Diana. His woolly blonde hair was the same angelic gold as hers but tinged with the fumescent effects the sun has on hair that surfs. Confident and supremely fit he strutted past me and I couldn't help but notice his gluteal masculinity which could have balanced a champagne glass on each buttock without the slightest spillage. Apparently, it takes a big hammer to drive a long nail.

Diana's eyes were locked on his and she smiled wider as he approached. I played a Prince number and they embraced and shared the warm halo that surrounded them. My chances with Diana were disappointingly grovelling in the sewer of my delusions as I rose to take solace in the sanctity of the poorly sanitised gentleman's room.

The squeaky tap bled some discoloured water into my cupped hands as I tried to focus on the serious teregian slowly invading my good eye. In the dim squinted light of the bar I probably looked ten years younger but with the water splashing on my face I hoped to rinse out a few crow's feet and wrinkles and restore my adolescent Adonis looks. The same blurred figure appeared in the mirror with a downtrodden bleak and weak smile as the door was kicked open with such intensity that I momentarily slipped forward, grabbed the sink for ballast and smashed my mouth on the stained and cracked porcelain and watched blood trickle down the lips of the Picasso in the reflection.

"This shit is too easy," yelled the Ram. His hands simulated a flurry of quick movements meant to imitate the 'No Kan Do' style of close contact annihilation. "Woo!" he echoed through the piss stunk room.

I salvaged my dignity by weakly echoing his 'wooo' with a bloody- mouthed and sardonic 'Wooh!'

He strode past me and pissed long and hard into the cubicle toilet like a steroid laden horse after race day at Caulfield. He then sidled up to me at the sink and slapped me so hard I nearly spat my bloodied tooth into the pitiful image that sneered back at me.

"She's a doll isn't she?" he said patting his blonde locks and beaming his big white grin into the mirror.

"An angel," I gurgled playing with my last good eye tooth. He glowed with the confidence of a Greek god about to unleash his fecundity on the world.

"Play us a song piano man," he said slipping a crisp twenty dollar bill in my top pocket. "How about some 'Ace of Bass' buddy."

I could tell his taste in music was limited to what he'd heard in Lombok night clubs and matched the garish gold chain around his neck.

"I'll see what I can do Ram," and smiled pathetically at him as he strutted his butt out the door.

I patched myself up and reluctantly returned to the piano licking a swollen lip which would seriously hinder my singing but decided to fulfil my pre-paid request and belted out, 'All that she wants, is another baby' but it came out like it was being sung by Elle McPherson; All vat she vants is anover vavy…" The Swedish writers of that song would think I was taking the piss, but I had no choice.

Much to the pleasure of the Ram and Diana, they danced lasciviously close to each other and he bent her over the end of the piano and kissed her. She responded by lifting one of her shapely velvet-skinned legs over his prominent posterior and running her fingers through his fleece of golden hair.

Al watched from the bar realising his expensive stolen champagne had worked its magic after only one glass but not to his advantage. He tried to salvage what was left but the cork wouldn't fit back in the bottle. He gave up, raised the bottle to his lips and drank long and hard til it foamed out of the corners of his mouth and through his nose. We both watched as Diana and the Ram left through the swinging doors with their hands firmly planted on each other's arses smiling lustily into each other's crystal blue eyes.

My swollen lip felt like an extra thumb so I played an appropriate instrumental tune by Miles Davis called 'So What'.

I looked at Al and he shrugged at me through watering eyes, the expensive champagne still in his hand and a look of defeat pasted across his dial. He said in a pissy voice, "The only thing I have in common with him is that neither of us likes beetroot."

I had to reply even though my bottom lip had expanded and given me the look of a forlorn child who had still not got a bike for Christmas.

"Well, you can beat an egg, but you can't beat a root."

I finished the song with a few randomly selected plinky notes and let my forehead fall onto the keyboard for the finale where I rested and sighed at another missed opportunity for real love.

What a fantastic morning this morning,
With the surf dragging folks from their dreams
Barrels and reos galore
While Jupes met her new Schnauzer friends

The fitness brigade was greatly increased
Knowing each day is getting two minutes shorter
The septuagenarians supported the café
And I kinda think they shoulda oughta

Cos one day I'll be them
And there'll be a young 50ish punk
Who's looking me up and down
Then I'll be the one who's the subject
Of a controversial social observation in Downtown Clown Town

But I'll be just happy to see the sunrise;
I won't be judgemental at all
And I'll live to a hundred and surf every day
Regardless of the expected social protocol

Another day began.

GOLDY 7

Asian Annie

She staggered in sheepishly hiding her eyes under a recently dyed maroon fringe. The leopard print dress hung from her broad shoulders with the disdain of a recently slaughtered beast. Her long legs were noticeably bandy, though I'm sure not from riding horses and she struggled to control the stilettos tied to her size ten feet. The rest of her hair was a recently ironed river of jet black oil flowing down her back. As she neared the bar her mascara-lined almond eyes revealed a distinctly Asian tinge. Her English wasn't too good and she handed Al a fifty as she ordered a 'cocktail'.

Al, not the best at mixing fancy drinks, asked "Mai Tai or Grasshopper?" He was hoping for the latter as that was the only cocktail in his repertoire.

"Glasshoppa good" she smiled through her thick black lipstick revealing a stupendous new dental miracle. Al got busy pretending he knew what he was doing. She looked around the dark space as though expecting someone and eventually spotted me and nodded kindly in my direction again revealing a wide white smile. I returned the smile careful not to reveal my poor oral hygiene and continued playing 'I think I'm turning Japanese'.

With some gingerly selected steps she balanced her fancy cocktail towards me and sat on the stool at the end of the bar behind me.

"You know Harry?" she said to no one. I realised she was talking to me.

"Harry Belafonte or Harry Chopin?" I said.

"No, Harry the Rat," she smiled again amused at my humour.

I knew Harry the Rat was a pimp in the downtown area but hadn't seen him for some time. He was bad news and had been kicked out by Al on many occasions. I played dumb.

"Never heard of him," I played 'Roxanne' just for the hell of it. She sipped her drink quietly as the song played out and Al kept a close eye on her. I went to relieve myself in the sanctity of the executive suite bathroom that Al called a toilet.

I jumped at the person staring back at me and realised I wasn't as good looking as I thought when I woke up this morning. My stubble was greying and the spider veins on my cheeks were reminiscent of an alcoholic Santa Claus. The water was cool on my face and neck and I pictured Burt Lancaster rolling on the beach in 'From Here To Eternity' but on second viewing I realised my low cheek bones and acne scarred nose wouldn't have got me the part. Despite that I was short and had a permanent inerasable scowl to my physiognomy. As I went to leave, the door pushed open and there stood Asian Annie, as I'd now nicknamed her, still holding her Glasshoppa in one hand and an unlit cigarette in the other.

"Got a light?" she asked smokily through the fringe.

I obliged and she continued to walk in on the recently mopped floor taking little steps on her high heels like a child learning how to ice skate.

She smiled again and blew smoke in my face.

"You want to have some fun, yeah?"

I blinked and checked my image in the mirror making sure she was talking to me. I shrugged at the guy in the reflection and said, "Yeah, why not, I've got nothing to lose."

She handed me her drink and then skated into the cubicle and had a piss while I stood listening and looking at her half-finished Grasshopper. She emerged with a cheeky grin and a pair of panties which she proceeded to place on my head, took me by the hand and led back into the cubicle and closed the door. It was awkward in that space to say the least. I was reaching up to kiss her when I heard two guys come in to the room outside and began pissing in the urinal. We could hear their blokey conversation when Annie grabbed my crotch and I realised her hand was bigger than mine.

"My god, that's huge," I said grabbing her hand and looking up into her eyes. She put my hand on her crotch and then I realised she was hung like a donkey. Of course, the broad shoulders, difficulty walking in heels, bandy legs; large feet and now that I thought about it a somewhat throaty voice emanating from deep within her Adam's apple. Even her knees were bigger than a Samoan rugby players'.

The two men at the urinal saw me rocket out of the cubicle looking surprised and sweaty, my fly undone and I proceeded to slip on the wet tiles and fall unceremoniously into the urinal where they were standing pissing. They turned to see Asian Annie slide up next to them, lift her dress and proceed to piss, again, while they zipped up, laughed and exited to tell the story in the bar. Asian Annie finished with a couple more squirts, smiled at me gently, picked the panties off my head and skated out the door with Glasshoppa in hand.

I crawled from the stink of someone else's urine and rolled onto the floor clutching a partially deteriorated toilet lolly in my hand. Was I so desperate for affection that I couldn't tell the difference between a real woman and a fake one? I had reached a new low but I tried to rationalise that it couldn't get any worse. Embarrassed to re-enter the bar, I climbed out the window landing loudly into a large mini skip full of rubbish that hadn't been collected for a week.

Several rats tried to fight me off from their booty and I slid awkwardly out of the bin into the alley at the back of Al's Bar.

My socks and shoes were squelching with piss and I could smell the rising odours of decomposing food coming from the pockets in my pants. Undaunted, I decided to walk to my apartment, shower, change and re-emerge for the last set if only to honour Al who I owed money anyway. I took my shoes and socks off and left them in the alley walking barefoot along the footpath sticking to gum and who knows what else along the way. I sat on the doorstep of a building to peel the used condoms and bubble-gum from my feet and massage them back to life as some passers-by threw money at me like I was a bum.

Half an hour later I entered Al's with a fresh suit and a shave resembling a forlorn Humphrey Bogart. I played as though nothing had happened. Asian Annie was gone and Al raised his hands at me as if to say 'where the fuck have you been?' I raised a thumb at him and smiled. He waved his hand at me and went back to the bar.

Trying to push the recent demoralising scene from my mind, I played Joe Cockers' 'Feelin Alright' when in walked Harry the Rat. Before Al or I could say anything he had emptied the contents of my tip jar into his hat and said, "I believe you owe me this for services rendered."

He pointed at the swinging doors at the entry and there stood Asian Annie blowing me kisses and smiling widely. Al looked at me with a 'wtf' look on his face and I smiled at him and played 'All of me, why not take all of me…' He waved his hand in my direction as if he didn't want to know and I certainly didn't want him to know.

Brazen youth basking in the rays of forgetfulness

Cautious pensioner imprisoned by adolescent memories

They're both connected along the same dotted timeline

One at the beginning

One nearing the end

Same changing skies

Night and day

What do you want to want?

Can we both learn from each other?

Or will wisdom wilt

As our memories melt

One heart burns out the sun

The other coddles the moon

In the quiet of the night, you lay in your bowery

Wakened by your random dreams;

That's who you are

A piece in the puzzle

A realization so humble...

Contented, you sleep

Youth and age forge on

Embracing the next dawn

Repeat...ad infinitum...

DRAWER OF MEMORIES

I keep all my memories in a drawer somewhere. Sometimes I open it and watch them fly out like faded butterflies trying to recreate the initial excitement that went with them and regain their colours but they always seem more faded when they reluctantly fly back in. Some memories have faded so much they cannot come out and have dehydrated into dusty stains on the bottom of the drawer. But they're still there, buried deep, never to fly again. Some of them bore too much hurt and lost love to be summoned into my consciousness lest it hurt all over again and cripple me with remorse. They stay hidden in the darkest back depths, away from the light, transforming into black moths of the night suddenly appearing when you least expect it and for a brief moment you acknowledge them and their power over you and you gently coax them back to their lifeless cave and close the drawer. The curse of memory can crumble the hardest man and send the most stoic woman to insanity. You cannot escape it! It is all around you!

Why do I have all these keepsakes, souvenirs, pictures, toys, art, books, nick-nacks, statuettes, vases? Most were given as gifts, some purchased on holiday and some were made by hand, by others and by me. All of them represented some strategic moment in time, a birthday, a romance, an appreciation gift and they all initiate memories, some less powerful than others, some feint and wispy, some sinister and menacing, some short and dull.

My eye is drawn to a flower about the size of my outstretched hand. I pick it up and feel the tiny dark pink (puce?) beads. Each petal is edged with a row of white beads and the centre, its' stamen and pistil, are also white. I remember my wife souveniring this unique piece of art from a trash heap thrown over the walls of Rennes Le Chateau. It was a discarded grave decoration callously thrown away when its' purpose had been served only to rot in a pile of forgotten memories.

It was hand-made by a villager, caretaker of some sorts, who tended the tiny graveyard. She had learned the art of making these seemingly eternal wreaths from her ancestors, from a collected memory. Hours of meticulous devotion and care tossed into the ether after being on display for a few months in a tiny courtyard in a tiny hilltop hamlet at the base of the Pyrenees. And yet thirty years later, here it was, in my hand.

The original artisan had expertly and carefully wired it together to make it pliable and attached it to a thicker wire with thread wrapped tightly into a strong wad. The wad was beginning to deteriorate now and the wire was rusty but it was still formidably beautiful. The beads, about 1mm thick, were perhaps a little faded but nevertheless intact. I straighten out the petals and pucker the centre spreading the interior into a symmetrical shape. It has been lying in a drawer for more than twenty years and it needs to regain its' initial beauty and shape under my careful hand. Originally it was one of many flowers attached to a larger bouquet made for a respected and eminent member of this tiny hamlet. When we found it, it was not near or on a grave so I know not to whom it was dedicated. Only later when I visited the graveyard on the other side of the looming wall did I see other such flowers similarly designed and adorning fresher graves. Was it a local tradition perhaps or a perpetuation of memory for the dead; immortal and beautiful? The discarded flower in my hand was originally meant for someone and whilst being made received the thoughts, the mourning, the loss and memories for which it was designed. Like a sacred rosary with each threaded bead containing a prayer, a meditation to soothe the sorrow of departure. Each bead representing a day in the life of the deceased, a mandala blessed with tears and love. Artful hands threading patiently to dispel the painful thoughts, a licked finger assisting the grasp of each tiny memory, the accidental spiking of the wire drawing blood from the sweaty hand and each spike brings physical pain masking the anguish in the mind like a punishment for sins yet unconfessed. And yet here it was, in my hand.

I wondered about its' shape and colours. Did they represent something mystical with the six petals and the five inner sepals around the central elliptical bud? Was it based on a flower that grew locally or did it represent an ancient biblical flower? Who designed 'the first one' and when was 'the first one' designed? What did they make them from before wire and plastic beads? Why spend so much time making them if they were only to be thrown away after a year or less? Why not real flowers which will naturally fade back into the ground? This was made to last and to remind people for a lot longer than flowers would and create a stronger, more permanent memory.

As I look at it more carefully and understand the design, I realise the petals were made separately and attached to the centre and the stem later. The thin wire cleverly threaded straight up the underside of each petal and a strengthening piece is added crossways halfway up to keep the shape. There is no evidence of the wire on the topside. It has been cleverly hidden so as not to detract from the finished beauty which will face the sun, the mourners, the onlookers or me. The only person who won't see it is the person it was made for.

The beads on the underside still have some of their original sheen and have not faded as much. The hidden art is underneath so as not to reveal its' deathly representation above; a skilful deception. What is underneath the radiant petals is the engineering, the life force that holds up the premise above, and not as the alchemists may claim, 'as above, so below'. Its careful trickery now revealed to me has painted it less ethereal, more mundane, ever more morbid than the grave it once adorned or the rubbish heap destined to consume it over time. And yet here it was, in my hand.

I see more imperfections as I look at the underside of one petal; a single green bead. I look for more but there are none. Is this a deeper esoteric inclusion signifying the day of birth or the day of death or had they just run out of puce coloured beads? Why green? Did it get mixed up in the vast jar of beads somehow and was absentmindedly threaded without thinking?

I sense an image of more than one woman, maybe a circle of them chatting while they work, maybe to nervously distract them from thinking about their own mortality. Frivolous talk of daily things, their families, their ancestors, their children. One woman is making petals and laying them on the floor in the middle of the circle. One is assembling the petals on the stalk with wire and thread; one is making the white sepals and pistils and placing them on the floor. One is sorting beads into colours and is distracted by a funny story about her eccentric uncle Leo and the green one goes into the jar with the others; maybe she was colour blind? Maybe this bead has no memory attached to it until now.

I alone have created a memory surrounding the green bead and it will now continue. It was supposed to be forgotten more than thirty years ago and, by now, would have eventually fallen from the rusted wire and disappeared into the earth in the south of France and from all memory. And yet here it was, in my hand.

I pick the flower up to look into the heart of the threads underneath and a loose rusty wire end spikes my finger and draws blood like a thorn from a rose. A tiny speck of red balls up on my finger. Will I get tetanus and die? Has the flower from the grave come to take me as well?

The red speck of blood is the same size as the beads and it stays that size neither growing nor shrinking. It is slowly coagulating in the dry air; a message from beyond, from the dark underside of beauty reminding me that I too am mortal. I'm tempted to dab it in the centre of the white pistil and thus somehow infuse myself forever in the creation of this unique relic of someone else's death.

Now part of me will always linger amongst the sweat, tears and blood that created it.

If scientists were able to extract DNA from this beaded trinket, could it reveal a connection between my bloodline and those who created it, the skilled grandmother with calloused hands, the granddaughter still learning to perfect her technique or the corpse who it was intended to remember. I renege; then I notice one of the pinkish beads has come off. Despite my delicate handling I have somehow now released a piece of the flower from its wire prison. Using my speck of blood I pick it up and it sticks firmly in the dark red, suddenly giving it new life and it sparkles more brightly in the light, bathed in life and no longer condemned to celebrate death. And yet here it was, in my hand.

I panic thinking other beads will follow suit and begin to slide off to freedom, and yet I cannot see where it came from. The loss of this one bead has not detracted from the overall beauty of this flower. There is no visible hole above or below that would suggest it was ever even part of the whole structure. As though a city of thousands had lost one of its' own and no one had noticed. Lost and maybe never remembered. I look at the blood-soaked bead as though it were the person who had been buried in that tiny graveyard. The flesh and bones disintegrating into the earth while the bead survived. It would carry that all-important genetic code of mine for many years if I placed it carefully into a sealed plastic bag and stored it in a freezer; alone and yet carrying a life signature indefinitely. Now completely separated from the village of beads it will carry another separate memory. As I had overlapped the memory of the artist who made this death flower and she had overlapped the previous artist, this bead will undoubtedly meet a new fate and create yet another forgotten memory. How long could it perpetuate its' morose message from the grave?

I place it carefully into a glass bottle which holds my pencils. The blood prevents it from making a tiny tinkling sound on the glass and it sticks to the bottom. It will dry and be stuck for who knows how long. It will be difficult to tip out unless a pen disrupts its' resting place and moves it and gives it life and movement again. Will I remember that it is there now that I have given it a place in my memory or will it fade into a dusty, worthless trinket in a rubbish dump, once again? And yet there it was, in my hand.

I pick up the flower by the stem now and look at the petals on top. They move, vibrating on the thin wires like a real flower in the wind. I tap one and the others move in harmony waving back at me in a nervous to and fro dance like lute strings sensing the harmonies of each other. Pluck one string and the others move in harmonic sympathy. Again, the design and engineering has allowed this seemingly lifeless art to imitate life. After all these years lying in a dark drawer it has not become jaded or melancholy but has persevered and still reflects eternal beauty. It is not stiff and static; it has movement and grace; its' petals reaching out to the sun and the wind as they had done many years before at the original grave site.

I think about the efficacious hand that eventually plucked it from its pride of place and tossed it cold-heartedly over the wall, a drop of some ten metres. Of course, it was attached to a much larger wreath then and we only took part as a memory of Rennes Le Chateau. It survived travelling around in our van and the plane trip from London and Portugal. It survived four house moves and was still not lost. It was shown to friends and family as an unusual relic of our mystical journey and provided us with interesting conversation pieces but eventually, its' magic waned and it was put into the dark drawer with many other long forgotten memories. And yet here it was, in my hand.

The death flower had lived on; beyond the unknowing recipient, perhaps beyond its' maker and certainly beyond other less dynamic souvenirs we'd collected. It was still telling its' story. Through me it had a life, a memory, a past and a future. Then I see more life emerging from the flower. I pick up the magnifying glass.

A tiny spider has built its' home in the relative safety of the death flower. I see tiny abandoned capsules lodged into the threads underneath. A miniscule network of food storage pods at the base of one of the petals now hangs pale with misuse.

The death flower had managed to provide a haven for life!

How many generations of this dainty arachnid had called this home; leaving the quiet and dark safety of the drawer to hunt for even tinier prey at night? Avoiding the geckoes that hunted them by hiding in the deepest recesses where the stem joins the sepal camouflaged as a white bead and too small to be licked out of its' hidey hole. Where did it come from? Were its' ancestors living there all this time? Did they crawl onto the death flower in the rubbish tip near Rennes Le Chateau? Is the spider from France? It survived quarantine inspections, heat, rain, darkness and possibly starvation. Was it already laden with baby spiders when we plucked it from the rubbish tip? Did it have a memory of where it came from? If the quarantine department read this would they come screaming around to assess and eradicate this tiny stowaway?

Even so, it is now part of my memories and I feel I should place it back in the drawer, in the darkness and let it reproduce itself indefinitely inside the death flower. How many generations of spiders had been given life inside the death flower? Would I interrupt this chain of events if I keep it out on show or would they adapt to their new surroundings as they had done for at least thirty years?

The flower is not affected by this occupation deep in its' bowels, in its' machinery of wire and threads. The spider deftly moves across the beads seeming to know exactly where to go. My breath temporarily sends him scurrying into the safety of the core so much so that I cannot see him anymore.

A once discarded relic of death containing the seeds of life; and yet here it is, in my hand.

I place the flower in the glass bottle careful not to disturb the blood soaked bead at the bottom. It is now on display permanently as a reminder of lost memories. Who would make my death flower I wonder?

I begin to retrace our mystical meanderings around Europe looking for the holy blood and the Templars. We were younger then, lovers on a whimsical quest being deceived at every corner by an elusive trail of historical crumbs and protected by the most unexpected angels of humanity. Our destination had always been Rennes Le Chateau; that mysterious hamlet where Berenger Sauniere had supposedly found unfathomable wealth and yet no one knew what it was or where it now slept. I was determined to find it; and I did, in a sense, find a rare treasure. We were never apart and we bathed in each other's presence as though we were the only two people in love on the planet, each containing one half of the other, our thoughts always intertwining like the petals of the death flower.

There were moments when we fought, disagreed and, at times, perhaps despised each other. Those memories were the 'dark moths' I didn't want to release from the drawer. I knew they were there but rarely wanted to relive those moments and yet now, as I'm writing, I have to, uncomfortably, revisit them briefly; perhaps as a cleansing or purging. I've done my contrition. For me, the black moths of the night were caged into the darkness, strategically inaccessible lest they take over and dominate and destroy all the beautiful moments we'd shared and send us down the path of self-destruction. There was too much good in what we shared for either of us to allow that to happen and so we buried them deep in the darkest recesses of the drawer. The memories we chose to share are the happy, exciting, smiling moments and we replay them to each other to ensure they are cemented into our memories keeping the black moths permanently at bay and perhaps, they will fade forever. Alas; they will always be landmarks in the journey of two souls.

Remember the cold nights in Scotland in the old monastery? Remember the fields of wildflowers in the van park in Arques and the underground river in Foix? You sat in the rose garden in the papal seat of Avignon. You saw the Templar graves in cold underground crypts and you walked the streets of Paris at midnight. The metaphysical bookshop that we could not find again and the murals of Nicolas Flamel on the walls of our neighbours' pension are engraved on our minds. This was mysticism multiplied by many millennia past and present and we were novices trying to unravel the mysteries of the future.

These are the memories most visited and reinforced in our collective psyche. The other darker ones are there but we don't let them out of their self-imposed prison. They're the only things that you hope will fade with time.

We never let them take over lest we forget what beauty we shared. What began as a treasure hunt revealed an even more profound and lasting beauty; love; our version of love, which to us was more deep and ethereal than any we had known before or since. A mutual respect and trust beyond doubt, freeing us to be who we really were, our spirits soaring, our souls irrevocably connected, our smiles never waning and our need to be physically close; ever present. Our thoughts were always with each other and every moment of every day was filled with anticipation of our next embrace. Those memories always fly out of the drawer boasting their full colours, alive and unaging, carefree and innocent like a newly hatched Morpho butterfly. That is why we are still together.

As the Arabian proverb says, "All sunshine makes for a desert." We are human, we all have failings and we all make mistakes. How else can we learn? The dark moths are there to remind us, to teach us the difference between love and hate. All the tears and uncomfortable silences, the lies and deceptions, the paranoia and hopelessness, the arguments over trivial things which seem to embed themselves between us are the path to being eternally lost. When we have reached the lowest point where emotions are at their most devastating and we launch into accusative tirades amidst acid accusations and degenerations of each other's character, blame is tossed freely without remorse and then, spent, we recede into a silent indifference where there seems no solution will ever resolve the madness. We are now surrounded by the dark moths and they whisper their evil suggestions for self-preservation. 'Should we stay together? Will the hollow words, 'I'm sorry' be enough to remove the deep stain now etched in our memories? We can't look each other in the eye. We leave without a goodbye. Where will we go?' No-one can deny that they have never been to this point. The nadir is the lowest point; remember? If you don't learn from this, then you are lost.

Is this the final blow to the ego that has assaulted our dignity and self-respect and left us with a hollow heart and a vengeful mind? You cannot succeed unless you have failed many times. This is what our memory is for; to help us learn and to progress into the future with dignity, respect and humility.

What are the possibilities beyond this moment when tears have exhausted themselves through self-pity and the need to be alone and independent will assure that we will never be hurt again? Will the dark moths prevail and finally divide us so that our memories of each other will only be that horrible moment when we selfishly say 'No!' It is a powerful and truly demonic thought which bolsters your ego and prepares you for anything. Your resolve strengthens.

After a time of ruminating on the possibility of aloneness, perhaps forever, the angelic butterflies appear and they try to comfort you, chirping away at the moths, telling you that maybe it was your fault; it's ok to be wrong. Apologise and move on. Force the dark moths back into their lair. Learn from this moment. You don't want to admit defeat and you swallow hard wondering who will make the first move. Who will admit they were wrong first? This can't go on. It occupies your entire mind and it could destroy you.

The release of endorphins and serotonin floods through your blood and you pity each other. How could we treat each other like this? Am I really that bad a person? Is there not an ember of love burning which we could gently blow on to bring the roaring fire back? Are we not more mystically connected than anyone else on the planet at this point in time? Neither of us knows the truth.

Our saddened eyes meet; we awkwardly mumble an indistinguishable apology and embrace cautiously as if for the first time. Tears flow again but these are different tears, sweet tears, humbling tears. The embrace moves to swaying and whispered admissions of guilt and heartbroken admissions of love. We sway to a mystical dance that no one but us can hear. Between tightly squeezed eyes, forgiven regret flows down our cheeks and we taste our own salty tears, breathe a new air that heralds our future and all is forgiven.

The black moths are retreating, defeated by love, back into the drawer; banished, and new butterflies are born emerging from around us sanctioning a deeper love than ever before. A metaphysical transition of the soul that allows us to realise the alchemist's true meaning of the Philosopher's stone within each of us. Transformation. A hard lesson learnt and we continue, trying as quickly as possible to dispel all those recent emotions that sought to separate and destroy us. That is why we are still together.

I look into the drawer once more and see an odd shaped stone. It fits in the palm of my hand neatly. It is smooth and grey. I feel its lack of corners and look at the tiny striations embedded by heat from millions of years ago. I have no memory of this rock.

Is it mine? I ask my wife and she too has no memory of it and yet there it is in the palm of my hand. We discuss the possibility that one of our children collected it on a beach walk or in a stream in the mountains and then carried it home in their pocket and placed it in the drawer of memories. We have other rocks with distinct memories attached; the bloody stones of Montsegur, the ocean-smoothed granite rock we guessed was an aboriginal tool for crushing molluscs, the strangely coloured sandstone in the shape of a heart. But no, this one is unfamiliar. Did anyone remember where it came from? Did any of the children who are now adults remember putting it there? If I showed it to them would they suddenly realise the time and day they had chosen that stone over all the others along the shore front or from the creek near the waterfall?

It once was somewhere else. Created millions of years ago by a violent volcanic upheaval, cooled and shaped by the water and the wind before there was any such thing as memory, for memory is a purely human creation. Yet if it did have a memory what would it have seen, heard and felt during those millennia of silence and stillness.

Anonymous amongst all the other rocks and stones it sat patiently, undisturbed and unaware of the ebb and flow of the tides, the violence and calm of the wind and the evolving animation of the creatures around it and long epochs of time marked by light and dark and light and dark. Unaffected by variations in temperature, it endured but not without consequence. The smoothness I feel was no doubt a result of the soft and continuous movement of water delicately rounding its edges taking small pieces away as it washed gently every moment of the day; waves licking rhythmically over and around sometimes pushing it to roll forwards and back over other rocks leaving a sparkling corrosive crust of salt as the tide moved back out leaving it motionless for another twelve hours. When it did move there was sound clunking a dull rhythm that no human would ever hear.

The sound of sand whistling stingingly across its surface like a timeless and inexhaustible grinder, the sizzle of dispelled heat when finally the ocean would cool it after baking in the relentless summer sun. It used to be somewhere else and now here it is in my hand. I have created a memory for it and it can now sit with the death flower on display. I have given it life though I know not where it came from or who plucked it from its original abode and carried it affectionately to the drawer of memories. It shall be my rock of the ages continually reminding me of the ancient past which no person will ever have a memory of.

I panic momentarily thinking of all the things that I may have forgotten; not just things but events, moments that I perhaps should remember. Surely no one can remember everything. It is not possible. And yet, with a visual stimulus or reminder from someone, some vague recollection seems to emerge. I have no memory of early childhood until I was four or five and they are short sketchy memories told to me by family or friends and reinforced by viewing photographs or home movies or hearing the same story from a dotty uncle or grandparent.

Their memories are forgotten too with only traces of legend surrounding their past which is also an overlap of my past and mine will overlap my children's' past and so on. What should I leave them to remember?

Which memories are important? How much that 'used to be modern' is now forgotten? Rubbish heaps all over the world contain the 'discarded present' and undoubtedly lots of knick-knacks and personal treasures which will end up in a pile of human non-memory or a future archaeologist's dream connection to the past.

As I'm thinking this a faded postcard reveals itself to me from the drawer. That's right, one of a whole pile of postcards as I remember which date back to the First World War. My wife found them on a rubbish tip in Carnarvon Western Australia and rescued them from permanent obliteration. She has carried them around for more than thirty years and we have often opened them and perused the personal correspondence between a young man at war and his sister. A few may have been addressed to a sweetheart who waited for him but most were addressed to 'sis' but we know from the address that her name was Miss S Ward, 'Sally' as we called her hence forth.

In those days family photos were sent as a postcard and were the only form of correspondence between distanced family members. From the cards we recreated the events surrounding their lives. Sally moved from Tottenham or Wigan to 370 William St Perth. Cards were sent to her from T. Healey aboard SS Armadale and contained brief but heartfelt messages hoping to be remembered. One such card says, 'As through the world I wend my way and many changes see, T'will cheer my heart to know each day, that you'll remember me.' June 10th 1913. Another saying, 'I hope you will keep this card.' One card has a picture of a young girl lying in the back garden holding a large black cat and on the back, 'These have all been taken in the yard. This is our old cat Nellie. Will you write?'

Another unsigned card has a photo of a young girl standing on a chair which was taken at Electric Studios. She is seen in a white dress of the era trimmed with lace and a similar white matching bonnet, long white socks and of course her best dress shoes with little pom poms. The chair is an exquisitely carved Victorian piece with turned legs twisting up to an ornately decorated seat and backrest. These cards were sent so that no-one would forget. So Tom and George would not be forgotten even though they may have perished in the war: If they had survived, like the mail, it would have taken months for them to return home. Hundreds of cards sent to Sally back and forth so their memory would not be lost.

Someone had dumped these postcards at the tip in

Carnarvon. A niece or nephew who had come to clean out their deceased aunts' house and had no interest in keeping the memory alive and yet, they survived. Somehow they were rescued from total obliteration and now I'm holding them in my hand. What was once intended to be forgotten had new life. They are part of us now and as important to remember as the rock and the death flower. Some of them have become quite collectible as they were coloured and embossed with beautiful images of the turn of the century landscapes and architecture. Although they used to belong to Sally as a keepsake, a link to love over a vast distance, they are now also an intriguing part of our own memories and they will sit next to the rock and the flower. Though I did not know them, Sally and George and Tom will not be forgotten. I pick a few well-chosen postcards and place them near the rock and the flower.

I realise that so much has passed into history that will never be again. Recently, at a gathering of friends, we shared jokes. I had one new one to share but all the other myriad of laugh-out-loud jokes and stories I'd heard over the years had completely gone. Did you hear about the two nipples that got kicked out of the bar? They were off their tits!

The harder I tried to think of a joke the less success I had apart from a few corny old school yard jokes and 'Dad jokes'. I could not recall any of consequence that would have everyone in stitches. I briefly entertained the possibility of early Alzheimer's but soon realised everyone had similar difficulty. It was not something that was necessarily burned into our memories and many jokes were forgotten like deleted E-mails. We could all remember recent personal events and the latest news items and what they had for breakfast and maybe their pin codes and the number plate of their car but these were necessary memories unlike emotional memories where feelings were attached. Events which have emotional content stick harder in our memories than anything else.

Those elated moments my wife and I shared during our trip to Rennes have permanently lodged themselves in our long term memory and we will carry them forever.

I wonder if our memory bank can get full after a certain time and if new ones replace older less important ones. If it gets too full do we stop remembering? I think not. Our brilliant minds have unlimited capacity to absorb everything we see or do. Every smell, every touch, every taste somehow leaves its impression. If you are blindfolded and someone puts food on your tongue your memory instantly connects the experience to all previous flavours. The scents of a rose, a frangipani, a gardenia are all instantly recognisable based on what you have stored in your memory.

I glance at the drawer again and an odd shaped key ring forces me to look twice. My memory instantly floods with images of where it came from but then I wonder why I've kept it so long. Attached to the generic silver chain and loop is an oblong plastic container about 7-8cms long and 3cms wide. It has a brightly coloured logo saying 'Good boys cover up'. The bottom slides open to reveal a condom neatly packaged inside. I slide it shut again and journey back to the camp ground at Versailles. We were leaving our van there with the intention of staying in Paris for a few days. We were to leave the next morning and wanted to tell a neighbouring camper to watch it for us.

Not far from us, a group of young Brits were setting up camp for the night. They were from the Harlow Basketball club spending the weekend playing fixtures against local French teams. They were all typical lads, one a policeman, who decided to make a boys weekend of it and camp in a large tent about thirty metres away. There was ruckus and laughing and farts and burps and beer. They even bought their own blow-up doll mascot which they posed in different positions for photo opportunities, one with the doll's hand strategically placed down the trousers. They made first contact because we had a

GB sticker on our van and they asked us where we were from.

They warmed to us and offered us beer when they learned we were from Australia and asked us if we knew their friends from Sydney. Sorry, no we don't.

Later we went to a local restaurant and I was abhorred to hear them complaining that the waiters should learn to speak English.

"We are in France you know, maybe you should learn to speak French," I suggested. They wouldn't hear of it replying, "They bloody know what we're saying don't they?"

Nevertheless, on our departure the next morning they assured us they would watch the van and three days later, on our return, they welcomed us like old friends making jibes about the cuisine and the 'the bloody cars n what'. That night they had a campfire and decided to liven up the quiet campground with some hijinks after they'd had a couple of beers. One of them rolled up some newspaper, stuck it up his arse, lit it on fire and ran around the camp until the flames got too close and he swore and ripped it out and flung it at an elderly couple who were peacefully enjoying the spring evening. The blow up doll now had a name and made several more lude appearances before we returned to the van.

As they said their hung-over farewells the next morning they gave us some Harlow Basketball club stickers, a pennant and the cleverly packaged, socially conscious condom key ring. None of them had managed to use one on their boys' weekend so they employed them as novelty balloons and gave us the last one which I now hold in my hand. Despite their crassness and over-the-top antics and obvious racism, the memory has stuck with me. If I could have chosen to purposefully forget any event it would have been that one but they were harmless and besides they watched our van while we were in Paris.

After twenty years and several house moves I had somehow kept these items. Why didn't I throw them away? What sentimental value is there in keeping such banal souvenirs? Sometimes you cannot choose which memories will stay. Even if I had thrown them away, the memory would stay.

I have decided not to place it near the rock and the flower on display and I'm not going to give it life beyond its inanimate plastic packaging. Much like its contents, indeed, it prevents life at all and yet here it is in my hand. Too late; it is written and now qualifies as a memory as useless and facile as it is. However, I have removed it from the drawer and placed it in a storage box. I will probably have to revisit this memory at some time in the future when I open the storage box but now that it is written I won't have to dwell on the memory before I decide to throw it away never to be seen again by human eyes. But will I throw it away?

If only it were that easy. Remove all the unwanted memories, those sad moments that brought you down to an empty shell, the horrific ones that made you wish it wasn't happening to you, the times you were trapped in a scenario you had no control over. If only you could delete them forever. But would this change the way you are and would everything be eternally happy? Isn't it those memories which have given you a thicker skin, given you the tools you need to survive in the harsh realities of the world, given you a reference point so they don't happen again. Perhaps those dark unwanted memories in the drawer are meant to be there. They are yours and as much as you wish not to dwell on them, they are there for a reason; to protect you from making the same mistakes, to reassure you that things do get better and you can move on with your life. If you dwell on them, the dark moths will conquer you and you will subside into a fathomless pit of self-pity, remorse and anguish from which you may never recover. Through them you can become stronger by conquering the very fear they induce. They teach you coping skills and each time you have to use those skills you get better at it.

This is not to say you would go looking for bad things

to happen so you can practice your coping skills but it can be reassuring, when something does happen, you are better prepared for it because you have a memory of those dark moths in the drawer.

I scan the drawer again and see a tattered envelope which has been eaten by cockroaches. I slide it out from underneath the other trinkets and open it cautiously. Another memory I should have chosen not to keep.

As I read a wave of emotion flushes through me as much as when I first read it thirty-four years ago. A court summons for possession of a prohibited plant, namely, cannabis.

I remember how my younger self felt when I realised what this meant, what consequences would emerge in my life from this. I start to shake and I am angry and ashamedly bitter all over again. I remember wearing a tie to court thinking this would reflect my upstanding status in the community, my sobriety, my intention to conform. I remember feeling the embarrassment in court having my 'caring' $100 dollar lawyer promise I was seeking work at some supermarket chain and promising not to do it again. The feeling of complete blankness of mind when I was fined and convicted, a record for life was now revisiting my present psyche. I could tell no one; it was my secret. Some people still don't know, until now. I did not talk about it to friends or family and tried to put it deep in the drawer in a separate locked box, but it haunted me, gave me doubt about my future.

I painted myself as a failure and my frustration grew and festered until I thought I would never be able to achieve my goals in life, never be respected by anyone. For a long time I felt shame. Hadn't I cooperated with police, hadn't I admitted it was mine? I told the truth and that should stand for something. The miniscule amount I relinquished was a few stalks and some dried up leaf, barely enough to pack a cone and yet my life was now incontrovertibly ruined.

My flatmate at the time was caught with 15 Buddha sticks

and three bongs but because of his wealthy father he was acquitted of all wrong. He'd hired a top lawyer (who happened to be a heroin addict and died soon after) and continued his tertiary education without a conviction or fine. Injustice!

I felt robbed of my life. I ran away to the coast with my American girlfriend who was also implicated in the fiasco. I caught sand worms for the local bait shops and worked as a kitchen hand for a catering firm who knew nothing about my past. I was hiding from my real world and the shame it would bring. The pain of guilt festered and I tried to forget it and move on but I was haunted by my seeming failure and could see no way out.

I look at the letter again and wonder; if this didn't happen would I be who I am today? Would I have fought back so hard to prove myself to everyone I cared about. If this didn't happen could I have mustered the strength to succeed and fulfil my goals or would I have wallowed in my safe little world of obscurity and insignificance? This may have been the catalyst to spur me on, to encourage me to try harder, to seek out my dreams no matter what the obstacles. At the time I would have liked to airbrush it from my history but now I think it gave me strength and an indomitable confidence. I pushed myself to conquer my fears and become a self-made man and eventually proved to myself that I wasn't a failure, that I was worthy of respect and that I had something positive to contribute to the world.

I am still doing just that as I write these words. If not for this letter I may not have achieved all the wonderful memories that now crowd my consciousness. That letter which was so foreboding to me all those years ago was inadvertently a launching pad for the rest of my life and now here it is in my hand. From adversity comes wisdom; one would hope.

Aesthetically, the letter didn't look right beside the flower and the rock but I decided not to throw it away and slid it back under the other trinkets with the thought that I may take it out again in another thirty years and have a chuckle about my scandalous youth. By then, all judgement would have faded, all remorse would have diluted amongst the thousands of memories to come and it will pass into history and become a footnote on my genealogy.

As I withdraw my hand from the drawer I brush against a spiky straw coloured ball about the size of a tennis ball. There are two of them. I carefully pluck them from the drawer and place them on the table in front of me. The larger one is ragged and a little misshapen. There are strands of grass and sticks poking out like a hurriedly made bird's nest. I wonder how old it is. We called them sea balls because they were found on the beach. I hold the larger one up to the light. Where did it come from? How did it start? Was it a lump of beach grass that rolled along the sand collecting other pieces of flotsam and jetsam? Was it blown into the ocean and rolled around in the surf for years and then unceremoniously dumped on the sand again only to be rolled along another beach and then collected by its' mother ocean once more? Where had it been? How many miles had it travelled, propelled by the wind and tides? And yet here it was in my hand.

On closer inspection I can see sticks the size of toothpicks that may have been the root of a tiny mangrove, tiny conical shells still reflecting light from their pearlescent exteriors, indiscriminate lumps of hardened woody vegetation, delicate sea ferns cleverly intertwined in the grass, stiff filaments of brown coral poking through the edges of the ball. I'm tempted to peel it open like an onion and look deeper into its core but then it would be no more. All the time and memories tangled up in that eerily spherical shape would be undone just to satisfy my curiosity. I poke my finger into the centre without damaging anything and realise it is quite dense despite its' outward frailty. Years have made this ball. It is inanimate but contains memory. It is lifeless and yet supported life; tiny crustaceans, sea lice, polycystins, perhaps a raft for ancient stranded microscopic bacteria.

I don my special lenses and look deeper and find myself in another world. What appears to be a randomly massed together pile of sticks suddenly reveals a pattern intricately chaotic and ordered at the same time as though the cosmic plan had enacted itself here as much as it does in the far reaches of space.

Criss-crossed and thatched, some thicker, some as fine as hairs, some flat and striated, some curved, some straight but all part of the whole.

There are remnants of a faded leaf clinging like a fly wing and a larger, less aged leaf skewered on to the ball by several stronger spikier blades. Strips of seaweed 1mm thick and a miniscule finger of coral wrapped around a wiry branch of some indiscriminate fossilized marine vegetation present themselves for inspection. Then through the lens I see the ball of my biro starkly huge against a fine strand of grass and on it there is a tiny colony of spider eggs strewn across an even thinner filament of webbing. If my pen nib is 1mm across, these eggs are one twentieth of that size. More evidence of life and deeper memories attached to the sea ball.

Another thicker piece of vegetation appears through the magnified lens and appears to have salt crystals attached and glinting in the light and then I see it. The finest of all threads, bright blue but so thin I can hardly feel it between my now gigantic thumb and forefinger. It is so out of place and yet an intricate part of the ball weaving its way through to the core. I dare not pull it from its long penetration of mystery and history. Then, another green piece of fishing line brightly coloured and less worn, then, I see a thicker clear nylon piece just below it obviously older than the other two, maybe pre-war. Somehow, all three filaments of nylon had been picked up by the sea ball, all perhaps from separate anglers who had lost their line in a snag. All the fishermen may have memories separate to the ball but now they were part of it.

For all the years of rolling through the wind and bobbing in the sea, for all the creatures that inhabited it and all the plants and coral and seaweed that constructed it were contained in the memory of this ball. I could look into its' past and see where it came from and somehow it came to me and, now, I hold it in my hand; a ball of memories?

I place it carefully next to the flower and the stone knowing that at some point in the future I will want to look at it again and discover memories yet to be revealed. As I move it some pieces fall off onto the desk and I realise my close examination has taken away from the completeness of its memories. I mentally apologise and reach for the other smaller ball.

This one is different. It is smaller and more compact and there are no spiky bits sticking out. It is more spherical than the spiky one and I assume it as a much older, much more travelled and evolved version of the other. It is covered in fine hair-like strands and much more resistant to the inquisitive pressure of my fingers. My wife found it in Gawler at the mouth of the Murray River in South Australia in 1976. My dumb phone beeps a text alert.

As I write this I am drinking a St Hugo Shiraz Cabernet 2009 from South Australia. The phone beeps again. It's a text message from my learned scientist friend in Brisbane. 'The orange moon is nearly finished'. The lunar eclipse has nearly passed without my notice. I race outside and capture the shadow of the earth passing across the moon in an eerie orange glow. I have just captured a future memory for all to remember. It is 6:15 pm on the 15th of April 2014 EST (yes, check your calendar) and I'm seeing something that millions of people on the earth are seeing. A rare event and yet by tomorrow, maybe forgotten in most people's consciousness. By Thursday it will be as forgotten as George W Bush or the wise sayings of Paris Hilton or the proof that aliens have advanced our planet. Yet something rings true to me at this moment of witnessing a celestial milestone. The earth is shadowing the moon and I wonder which part of the earth is being projected onto the dark side of the moon as the earth slowly turns in space. Is it the northern hemisphere; the coast of Spain or the mountains of Canada slowly creeping across the face of the moon at a thousand miles an hour?

The moon is uncannily the same shape as the sea ball I've been studying so intently. The moon is round, supposedly because of its constant trajectory around the sun forming it into the orbital shape that it is now. The sea ball is the same shape and was formed from years of rolling and collecting and abrasion against the elements but if there is no air in space, if it's a vacuum, what's eroded the moon into the shape it is now? Do bits fall off it the same way bits of the sea ball fall off as it makes its' epoch journey around the planet. Surely, something is dislodged in a big sea, a cyclonic wind lifts it into the sky in a watery spiral and there is a trail of lost destruction and the end result is a more polished, more refined globe of memory. Are we not all like the moon and the sea ball as we travel through time and space? We lose bits and we gain more bits but it is always a more efficacious ball that we find ourselves rolling around the planet; smoother and more efficient than we have ever been before this moment. I digress as a result of the St Hugo and decide to return to the sea ball's microcosmic secrets.

If I were to say it looked like fine coconut coir I would be close but the fibres are as randomly matted as the spiky ball. If it has been floating for many years then it could have come from anywhere in the world, full of forgotten memories of long journeys, visits to deserted islands, wild encounters with hurricanes and violent seas and yet always resiliently floating on the surface, buoyant and mobile. Has it ever been held in another human hand? Has it been poked by curious turtles or tossed by playful dolphins? Once again I have the urge to surgically cut through it with a scalpel and see what's inside.

Does it contain the secrets of the sea or a hidden treasure? And yet here it is, in my hand.

It is a good fit in my palm and I imagine tossing it to someone who is holding a cricket bat. What would happen? Would it eventually fall apart or have the years and years of rolling made it impervious to damage? Could an ancient Indian child have picked it up as a toy and thus began the first game of catch?

I don my lensed cap again and look into the ball trying to penetrate its' mysterious soft veneer. There is evidence of larger flat pieces of grass, specks of shell being imprisoned by the fine fibrous hairs. A tiny tubular stick-like shape protrudes suggesting there is more of it hidden inside. Again, I resist the urge to pull it out lest I disturb its' ancient perfection. It may be a previously undiscovered species of coral or it may contain DNA from a prehistoric fish or evidence of life before oceans covered the earth.

There are small fingerprint sized depressions on the surface in a haphazard pattern, some slightly smaller or larger than the next. All the fingers that had pressed into its' impressionable surface perhaps, including mine? Small white specks, grey specks, specks of dust possibly accumulated in our house after it's' collection to our fold? One of the shiny black specks is a dead ant now entombed amongst the fibres destined to deteriorate into the depths of the ball and become part of its long memory. It's like looking into a head of thick, light auburn hair. Each strand is like a separate memory of its past. Millions of strands, like the moments collected in a lifetime all massed together in one ball of memory. If we collected every minute of every day and wadded them together it would still not come close to the intricacies of this enigmatic visitor from the sea.

It's not the only one I've seen. There must be millions of them out there still floating in the ocean or sitting on mantelpieces as a curio of some seaside village or rolling around the beaches of the world and yet here was this particular one which came to my wife at the mouth of the Murray. In fact, I remember her saying that someone else picked it up first, briefly looked at it and threw it back on the sand, discarded, like the flower, only to end up in my drawer of memories because it called to Donna. She gathered it subconsciously as a memory of Gawler. Or, it gathered her.

I now place it next to the shaggy sea ball and the flower and the rock and the postcard. It now etched itself into my memory. I think for a moment that I should release it back onto the sand where it came from and let it continue its journey and be discovered by someone else. After its long years of travel it has remained dormant, sitting in the drawer for ten years or more, a mere blip in its infinitesimal existence and I have stalled its' progress by keeping it as a curio to be admired infrequently for my own amusement.

Aristotle once said, "Memory is the scribe of the soul," and I think this is only partly true for there are things in one's life which are not part of the soul but of your heart and mind. Things that you would wish to forget because of their triviality or their misunderstood message to others. Memories can play havoc on the sensitive soul. Having too good a memory often plagues the innocent mind with visions of hatred and indifference, lost loyalties, mistrust and lack of appreciation for those genuinely honest things you thought you were doing. Too good a memory can reveal truths that no one wants to admit; images of events that others deny, conversations that were hurtful and now dismissed as lies. They only remain in your heart and soul and may never be collaborated by another even though it is all part of their somewhat dim and greying memories and for their own self-preservation they have buried them deep within the drawer, never to be exposed to the bright reality of the world again.

There is a map in the drawer. I recognize it as the map Gisbert gladly handed to me in Elmshorn on the 1st May 1993 when my wife and I were headed to Berlin. It was the day of the May Day protests which we were blissfully unaware of. He seemed happy to get rid of the map because it was so complex and difficult to read even though he was German and we spoke virtually none. Gisbert and his wife Verena had kindly put us up for a couple of days, then when we decided to leave for Berlin, he handed me the map saying he hoped it was more useful to us than it had been to them.

I unfolded it carefully and realized how very complex it was. This is before the days of sat nav and devices designed to erase your working memory.

The night before, Gisbert and I consumed a bottle of Greek Metaxa Brandy while we listened to David Bowie's 'Black Tie, White Noise' album. He asked me the meaning of life and I told him, 'just be happy'. He seemed content with that answer and rolled off to bed. The next day I was keen to get to Berlin and he had cheekily presented me with the most confusing map on the planet. It contained sections and subsections and fold out inserts and everything was a 'strasse' to us.

Between my wife's expert navigational talents and my skilful driving we found our way into Berlin but ended up on the eastern side of the recently demolished wall. I still remember walking out of the van straight into the Pergamum Museum and thinking that this was a Middle Eastern city transported holus bolus to the centre of Germany. Wow! Why? Was it war plunder? Was it believed to hold special significance to the occult obsessed fuhrer? Maybe there was something specific he was looking for that would give him an advantage over his enemies, a lost talisman that he would brandish before his armies to make him invincible. Whatever it was, it must have been lost in the memories of ancient history and handed down as legend and myth. Maybe it had been hidden safely in the back of an archaic drawer so as not to be accessible to people like him. Maybe he didn't have the right map to find it or he read it wrong and like us found himself on the wrong side of the wall looking for antiquities of magic and power only to find statues and artefacts that spoke of ancient Pergamum and which would ensure that no one forgot what a marvellous and grand civilization once existed there. Now, the Turkish city of Bergama sits atop its' once flourishing cultural site.

So the map led us to East Berlin and East Berlin took us back in time to ancient Pergamum and we looked at life-size statues depicting everyday life in the famous independent kingdom of West Asia in 283 B.C. When we walked out of the historic memories of the past we saw evidence of a wall that was recently demolished but the wall had left its impression on buildings with pale scars where it had prevented light since the 13th August 1961. But the wall was not forgotten; it held strong memories and still does. A man was selling tiny pieces of 'the wall' for 7 marks; a small piece of history with colours visible where a clever artist had painted clever political slogans and images to mark his disdain. But around the streets was a market; stall holders selling trinkets and records and eastern bloc home wares never before seen in Berlin. Art and memorabilia spanning the fifties, sixties and seventies were for sale as were retro collectables and previously unseen gadgets. Bakelite art deco vases, a rare doll, a belt buckle, a set of cards in Cyrillic were on sale. Trinkets and treasures were on display but they were from a different part of history which was thousands of years after thriving Pergamum.

The trinkets were all cheap and being sold in the city of Berlin which was established in the early 1200's and here we were as a result of a complex map, which I now hold in my hand. I place it back in the drawer to be discovered perhaps by someone in the future who has never seen a map and who may rely solely on satnav technology to get around; someone who has never had to memorize a landscape or remember an intricate short cut through suburban streets. When they have lost their ability to remember directions and only when the satellite fails and the technology has warped their sense of place may they need to consult this map for directions to the local supermarket in downtown Berlin. And yet there it was, in the palm of my hand.

What's this; an old tram ticket? I'm not sure why I have this. A small piece of paper about the length of a Bic lighter and about an inch wide flutters up as I replace the map. The paper is flimsy and the ink a somewhat faded blue. I can barely make out the printing and numbers but it looks like 'Valley to Kedron'. It may have belonged to my grandmother; a threepenny fare returning from an appointment in Fortitude Valley or a bingo game perhaps? The trams used to run in the middle of the main road and you would have to dodge traffic (though it wasn't that busy on the road) and sometimes jump on while it was still moving. 'Ding ding' meant we're moving again and a long leather rope inside would be tugged to halt the train when you wanted to get off. 'Ding ding'.

Nowadays, it seems a terribly risky way to travel especially getting on and off. The tram driver made sure all elderly people could alight safely and let it run just fast enough for everyone else to jump off without the tram actually stopping. There were no doors and lots of trust on the part of the passengers to actually get on in a split second. WPH&S would be mortified today to think of all the possible things to go wrong and yet thousands of people per day travelled all over the city evading cars and trucks and buses as they leaped off at their stop and crossed safely to the footpath, most times running to avoid being hit.

The ticket had punch holes in it and this validated your travel in case an inspector would mysteriously appear to check you had paid your fare. The conductor rolled out a ticket, punched it and handed it to you; and yet here it is in my hand.

I wonder how many of these still exist. Most would have deteriorated at a dump or blown along a street into a gutter and be dissolved in a deluge of QLD rain. Undoubtedly, there were enthusiasts who collected them and kept them as memories gone by. Some collectors may be looking for exactly this ticket to complete their collection.

The feel of the paper and the fading ink give it a nostalgia reminiscent of more innocent days; quiet Sundays, early nights, simple street lamps with yellow glows, early dinners and black and white newsreels on TV. No fast food, no flashing neon lights, no choking traffic and no one in a hurry to get anywhere fast. There were very few aeroplanes scarring the night skies with jet streams and thunderous roars. The ticket of innocent memories... Childhood walks around the suburb with no fear of danger, neighbours waving and saying hello, cubby houses in the mango tree, the distant smell of steak and three veg cooking in every household at the same time. My brother and sister and I could play for hours in the back yard with just a tea chest and some rope and our imaginations to amuse us. At tea time we would all reluctantly come inside, wash our hands and sit down to our meat and three veg with the possibility of home-made ice cream after we'd finished all our greens and then everyone tucked into bed before 10pm.

This ticket comes from that era of innocence and the memories it sparks are wonderful thoughts I wish everyone could have planted in their medulla oblongata. There was less judgement and more encouragement and tolerance of people and fewer expectations. There was discipline (mostly without violence) and respect for elders; honour and truthfulness were valued. There was an overall whimsical drifting as the school days seemed longer and weekends seemed shorter; sunburn was expected and cool breezes were welcomed in the sticky summer whilst sucking a mango seed in the shade of the jacaranda or Poinciana; simple pleasures for simple times. These are the memories cherished by the ticket of innocence and yet I am holding it in my hand.

The ticket deserves preservation and I place it inside a

dictionary to become a lightless lasting place to linger until the next seeker of memories looks longingly at its innocence. I place the dictionary in the drawer of memories with all its' own verbose memories. Fingerprints on the pages belying oily DNA from the distant past, assisting crosswords and homework and correcting love letters with eloquent linguistic literature and now it sleeps in the darkness with the ticket of innocence tucked deep in its' vast vocabulary.

Now I spy with my little eye, a red band made from woven cotton and nylon. It is small enough to fit around my wrist and has a silver buckle at one end. The first collar I bought for my dog when she was a pup. Jupiter didn't wear it much and it still looks quite new after nearly ten years. Of course she looked cute to us but did she remember it at all? What is in a dogs' memory? Is it the same as mine or am I just imposing my own memories of the collar on what I would like to think she remembers?

She remembers me and Donna and other people, even after months or years. Does she remember chasing cows and following chickens? When she dreams at night her little back legs thrust in mid-air and she winces quietly imitating a bark; an almost inaudible bark in her throat. Is she chasing or fleeing a foe or a friend? How far back does her memory go? In her dream she's running and talking at something, a rat, a snake, me on the beach chiacking around tempting her to come closer to the waves washing up the shore? Then she stops her innocent nocturnal meanderings and sleeps peacefully. Later, another memory infuses her with a flurry of faux barks and her tiny back legs move in unison recreating a moment that went before. A puppy chasing a ball with a flurry of larrikinism flashing her front paws out wide like a swimmer doing butterfly, running in circles with her cheeky eyes watching us laugh and her floppy 'Grommet' ears pegged back reflecting her playful mood.

Or is that just my memory of her? How would I ever know? Somehow the years have convinced us both that we share memories, people, food, places, other dogs and cats and now she is nearly ten, she speaks to me in what I can only describe as carefully undulating throatal phrases rife with intent and demanding as only an elderly canine can be. Where is my food? Why aren't you cooking dinner so I can get your leftovers? Bring my bed inside! Arooo! Arooo! If I say the words, 'go for a walk' her head cocks to the side and her ears go up and a sudden knowing in her eyes engages me to confirm the sounds by grabbing her lead immediately. Arooo!

She knows from her deep memory what those words mean; freedom, escape, a plethora of smells left strategically within her extensive olfactory sense tell a story left by others of her kind ; pooing in the wild and not in her backyard, leaving urinary messages to tell others that she exists.

The walk begins with a collar and a lead and the first one I bought her I hold in my hand. The red collar beautifully compliments her shiny black coat and white paws. She learns to stop at the lights, wait, sit; good girl. She has pleased you and listens to your tone. She faithfully stays with you and loyally protects you from everything and anything that may seem a threat. She is proud to wear the collar which makes her belong to you. She sits and smiles and pants and her tongue lolls out the side of her mouth and she lovingly looks at you. After the walk you take off her collar, pat her head and feed her the freshest meat which she devours as only a dog can. You place the collar in the drawer and she never wears it again. And yet, here I hold it in my hand.

Does she remember the collar? Somehow I know that if she smells it, it would conjure deep memories of her puppyhood and she will dream moments she hasn't dreamed for over 50 dog years and her little legs will run erratically and she will faux bark in her throat like an innocent child unwrapping Christmas presents. Dog memories..? I play with the collar momentarily and think of Joops as a puppy and then lovingly place it on the table next to the flower and the stone and the postcard. Arooo!?

A circular object about as big as my eye, metal, brown, brandishing the image of a king with a beard; Georgus the fifth, 1919. It's cold in my hand. How many hands have held this? Once, its value was contemporary and would have bought a week's food for a family of five. Where had it been in its ninety five years? What memories did it hold through generations? I remember now. My brother found it when he was digging up old pipes at Oxley in Brisbane. At the time, we surmised that it may have been dropped, lost by someone, a worker, a child, a drunkard, a soldier. Years of floods and silt, earthmoving, development, king tides and wind-blown erosion had buried it four feet into the clay. It had supposedly been lost and forgotten forever eventually becoming part of the carbonic sheath from which it came. But no; He found it amongst the muddy red clay when he was digging to repair a ninety year old pipe. A speck on the shovel saved it from its eternal grave only to share its memories with future generations; now revered as a reliquary of distinct importance, worth more now than it was when it was minted.

Not all that is old gains value as it ages; certainly not the perhaps hundreds of people who held it or spent it or flipped it for luck. The people who kept it in their pockets and purses, or banked it with bags of other coins would never be as valued or remembered as this coin was now or would be one hundred years from now. The dead are dead and the living march on. And yet here, now, I hold it in my hand and it marches on. I feel the cool copper and the raised lettering along the edge and the image of a once reigning king under the pad of my thumb. The people are all gone and forgotten but the coin remains and now it is in my hand. It travelled, it clinked, and it rolled and spiralled on the counters of countless hotels. Eventually, it fell and hid for who knows how long; and now I hold it in my hand. I place it near the flower and the stone and wonder where it will be in another ninety-five years in 2109.

If I aged as well as the coin I would be 144 in 2104. A projected future memory? I know it's not possible but if I give the coin to someone and they will it to their family, it may be valuable beyond expectations and provide one of my descendants with a large house and wealth. They may investigate where it originally came from and stumble across my name; resurrected in name only in 2104. Eccentric old Great Grandfather Estella; now there's a story! They may already have read the 'Drawer of Memories' which you are reading now and then decide to investigate what I did all those years ago and find a photograph and music and books and briefly I will appear again because of my connection with the coin which is now proudly displayed in an online numismatic museum.

The Death Flower had taken its memories far beyond its intended recipient; the stone had outlasted generations of evolving humans and the postcards have now extended the lives of Sally and her distant lovers. Whatever I give in this life will be echoed in eternity. My descendants will read this and it will become a reference point for their memories. What would I say to them?

"Hello Great Grandchildren of the future. Can you still read this language or has a new cyber language been invented where you only need a chip in your head to communicate with the global network past and present? Does anyone write letters anymore? Do you know what a barbeque is? When was the last time you hugged your family? Sorry, I'm being somewhat sceptical of the future. I would hate to think that technology has erased the family unit and made everyone isolated beings in a transient planet. Do you remember the coin; the one that made you so much wealth? It belonged to another era; an era before mine where money was earned and respected. Now it is the only one of its kind in existence. They can never make another. Just like me."

"How many phones have you had in the last three months? Are they still called phones? Does anyone still like flowers and trees? What season is it while you read these words? I hope its autumn or winter and you are surrounded by the auburn and red so prevalent at this time of year. The Poinsettias, the Poinciana, the Hippeastrums and the passionfruit are all blossoming now. It is cooler than expected this July with temperatures getting down to 2&3 degrees. The days are perfect with a cool breeze and a clear dry sky. The ocean sparkles through our polarised sunglasses as we sip coffee on the grassy headland and watch the surfers. The sun is warm and comforting and whales breach in the distant blue sea. What were you doing today before you started to read this? Do you remember? What legacy will you leave for your descendants? Ask yourself, 'Did you find happiness; did you give happiness to others?' This is what I give to you through the coin, not the coin itself."

I digress as my future descendants connect with the thread of 'The Drawer of Memories'. The coin has connected me ninety years into a possible future. If I flipped the coin out into my garden now, there would be no projected future as I had written it. There may be no descendants and no cyber chip in the head and no reason to look back at Great Grandfather Estella. Now there's a story!

I place the coin carefully beside the blood-soaked bead in the jar. They sit apart and silent in their new prison. No-one will touch them or look upon them or discuss them until I give them to someone else who will continue their memory, whatever that may be.

The drawer seems to be littered with detritus like any typical human household. Despite being closed for years, everything is covered in a fine layer of dust. Three and a half inch floppy discs, a plastic takeaway container filled with specially angle cut pieces of pine wood which were meant to reinforce a frame for a picture, a few rusted bull dog clips, a box of deteriorated rubber bands, a blue plastic peg, red and black permanent marker pens, biros, cassette tapes of Boz Scaggs 'Middle Man' and The Big Chill Soundtrack, a large wooden compass for drawing on a black board, a small double picture frame with nothing in it, two packets of photos from Suncolor Film Laboratory complete with negatives labelled 'Home Flora' and 'Art Photos', an empty cassette tape holder, screwdrivers that no longer fitted modern screws, a bone handled bread knife, a stained and faded Celco protractor, layers of sandpaper of varying grades, a roll of mysterious non-sticky brown paper tape, a black masquerade mask of a cat with white nylon whiskers, a plastic coin bag containing wax seals with the old English letter 'E' on it and some bronze ink, a wooden bowl containing rusted metal picture hangers and brass screw in eye hooks; an unopened packet of plastic stick on hooks for tidying away those messy bathroom items; a foam block print of the fleur de Lis, an old stapler, half a roll of dried up masking tape, a small messy roll of flimsy wire, an old milky plastic metric ruler, a small grey remote control handpiece for a portable boom box, a whistle containing a leather name tag that says, 'Ted', a half full 35 ml bottle of tape recorder rubber cleaner, part of a screw on easel support, an old plastic box containing a stainless steel compass for drawing circles, two boxes of staples; one with No.620 ¼" by Vanguard and the other with STAPLES AGRAFES 26/6 which are both rusted, full and unused. There is a yellow UHU glue stick amazingly not dried up, a small pair of pointed scissors, a rusted old divider (like a compass but with two points and no lead) for marking distances on maps, a special screw on needle nozzle for pumping up basketballs, a pair of electrical wire snips which have been missing from my pliers collection for years and a reasonably well-sharpened brownish colouring pencil broken in half. But to my amazement, my granddaughter Asha, has just discovered a five cent piece, a guitar pick and a metal and a plastic pencil sharpener. There is another ten cents found along with a pair of surgical bandage cutting scissors.

Then to my amazement I see two tiny puce beads, from the death flower, and as I look further more beads appear. Asha is picking them out of the drawer with her tiny fingers and she finds another ten cent piece.

"Look Poppy, it's another flower!" And sure enough it was; another part of the Death Flower. This one is completely different in shape and it has a darker blood red colour strewn through the cleverly designed leaf. There are clear beads around the outside, a slightly more lilac inner margin and then the blood red beads loop around the wire stem. Some of the outer beads appear to be orangey but I can't work out if that's the clear beads affected by light and faded or if there is a core of colour inside them. My wife astutely points out that the orangey colour is the rusted wire inside the clear beads. She likes the colour created by the flowers natural attrition; clever girl. The messy underside construction belies the craft used to hide the mechanics on the top of the flower but again, I pick up the rusty wire and am spiked by the thin support wires underneath. Will I get tetanus out of this stabbing or will I be immune to the Death Flowers' second attempt to take me to the grave?

I realise all these things in the drawer have not been touched or used or looked at or examined for ten years or more. What are they doing in the drawer? Are they just filling the space so we don't have empty drawers or are they something we don't want to discard yet? The only thing I want to dwell on or keep is the new part of the Death Flower. Each time I pick it up the small sharp piece of wire at the back of the stem reminds me how dangerous it could be. I think of its' creator again and look at the ancient meditative perfection that went into its' birth. It is the only thing I take out of the drawer and I place it reverently near the other flower on my desk complimenting the larger death flower petal with its centimetre diameter leaves blended to look like a fading leaf in the last throes of autumn, mimicking death and yet it has survived at least eighty seasons without losing its' beauty. A memory only just rediscovered and yet there it was in my hand. I had no memory of this second piece before now and I wonder if there are more pieces somewhere I have forgotten.

Later, my wife assures me there were other larger pieces which have since been discarded when we moved house. It was a moment of ruthless cleansing to reduce the baggage we were carrying around with us, to reduce the clinging unnecessities of life that had somehow glommed onto us.

The other pieces of the flower had gone to find their own destinies perhaps again in a rubbish dump or fortuitously rescued by a nostalgic soul who thought the same as my wife did when she first discovered the death Flower in Rennes Le Chateau. That soul may have seen something unique when everyone else saw a tawdry piece of junk. They may have it displayed in their house as a mysterious link to the past which they had desperately tried to research with no luck whatsoever. They may have kept it just out of curiosity and gained some psychic link to the deceased person for whom it was intended or the artisan who lovingly created it to perpetuate a memory.

All those junky things in the drawer were connected to someone's memory but not all to mine. Some were just randomly tossed in there to store because they may be useful stationery items or may become valuable collectibles in the future. When will a Boz Scaggs tape become a museum piece? When will anyone value a rusted pair of dividers to on-sell to an avid cartographic enthusiast? If I place the drawer back in its' carefully measured guides now, how long will it be before I decide to look at it again? The next time I move? A frantic and callous spring clean one day when I'm feeling particularly concerned about the unnecessary baggage I've accumulated? Now the whole drawer is in my hands containing all the previously described items less the ones I have chosen to display on my desk. The ones that carry the strongest memory will stay. The rest will be tucked away for a future ponderance.

Just as I slide the drawer back into place I see a thin plastic coated piece of paper about the size of a wide bookmark. It had been camouflaged from my view along the inner edge of the drawer until now. I gingerly take it out and notice the amateurishly sticky- taped cover of crinkly clear plastic that makes a crinkly sound when you touch it. I flip it over and see a souvenir bookmark woven in Toowoomba.

It is a black and white depiction of the United States 'Eagle Landing Module' with Neil Armstrong and Buzz Aldrin setting up experimental equipment on the moon's surface in the foreground. It says, 'Moon Landing' by astronauts Neil A. Armstrong, Edwin E. Aldrin Jnr., Michael Collins, July 1969. At the end of the pennant is a bright blue nylon tassel typical of the era. It is obviously an extremely collectible piece of space race memorabilia and yet here it is in my hand. My wife claims to have bought it in an op shop in Caloundra for no other reason than she thought it might be an interesting collectible curio. The coincidence is that it is the 22/7/2014 today and the commemorative forty- fifth year of the moon landing was celebrated yesterday in the press and media. People have been ringing the radio station to relay their personal childhood memories of the moon landing watching it on black and white TV as Walter Cronkite narrated the historical moment for mankind like it was a sporting event. This souvenir bookmark has appeared at this moment to remind us of what we had achieved before the invention of social media. Apparently many millions of people were tuned into the same broadcast at the same time and this still holds the record for viewing audiences worldwide. This is a moment in time which may fade into obscurity as much as Captain Cook's discoveries or Tesla's influential futuristic experiments while we delve deeper into the cosmos and try to escape the inevitable destruction of our planet earth. Or maybe the sceptics will prove the moon landing was really a hoax? Heavy!

The souvenir bookmark which I hold in my hand is now carefully placed into the dark verbal recesses of the dictionary where the innocent tram ticket resides. It is safe from the destructive ultra violet light and will be preserved for future generations to discover, perhaps at the same time as the coin?

I close the drawer and return to the laptop keyboard somehow recalling the recent giant moon (yes, check your ephemeris). It was huge in the eastern sky as the sun set in perfect synchronicity in the west. The landscape on the horizon added depth, size and colour as the pinky geo-satellite rose imperceptibly into the cool mauve night sky. Sadly, the moon is slowly moving away from us by a centimetre or so a year, so eventually the perfectly sized eclipse of the moon over the sun will be no more; but not in our memories.

One of the families who witnessed the lunar landing in 1969 ran outside to see if they could see the astronauts on the moon. I wonder how many people nowadays would be that naïve about science and the way things work. Wasn't that a wonderfully innocent time when people believed in seeing to believe. One viewer watched the landing on a 1960's designed space helmet TV. Cool! 2015 is the year the 'Jetsons' cartoon was set in. Where's my flying hydrogen car? Where is the instant food from a machine in the wall? Where is Rosie the loveable, tireless, patient robot?

Actually, the Jetsons had a skype machine where you could talk to people and see their faces. That was in a time when only telephones were the modern form of communication. Treadmills to walk your dog or exercise; yep we have those now. Microwaves, blue tooth technology, radar scanners, scammers, satnav, black boxes, smart rockets, I-pods, I-pads, smart phones, dumb phones and search engines are all part of our technology which didn't exist when the Jetsons were conceived. Has this made us more connected or more isolated. Divide and conquer? Are we separated from each other so much so that we don't have to talk face to face anymore and embrace as humans were meant to do? I don't like it! I don't like it at all! (Mr Horse)

I digress once again into a combination of futuristic fantasy, reality and memories. All this from one drawer and yet I wonder how many of these drawers exist in billions of homes across the planet. Do you have one of these drawers of memories which you can use to link you to your past? Go to the third drawer in your kitchen and see what's in there; things you haven't touched or used for years and yet you keep it for that one moment when guests arrive and ask you if you have a bean stringer. You proudly present the bean stringer and also proudly say you have never used it to string beans and you suddenly relay the story of where it came from, partly as an excuse for having it in your drawer and partly because of the nostalgic history which is attached to your memories of it. See, you can't escape the drawer of memories. Every time you open a cupboard or drawer it contains memories which are attached to the items you have stowed there. The recently purchased spice grinder has as much memory as the coffee machine or the bean stringer. Where will your bean stringer be in ninety years? The bean stringer is a redundant technology not only because we no longer have stringy beans but also because, nope that's it, we no longer have stringy beans. I think we should call the original manufacturers of the bean stringer and ask them to recall all their models from origin to the late 1970's, unclutter people's houses of these now useless gadgets and dispose of them in the most ethically responsible way possible. A big hole filled with bean stringers may be found by a future archaeologist and he would gain a glimpse into our society and what we didn't value enough to keep. Now let's get started on all the other useless gadgets we thought we really needed in the past twenty years that are taking up valuable space in your garage where a perfectly good Ab Pro 3 could be sitting or a Bullworker?

What's a Bullworker you may ask? I had a friend who had a Bullworker. It was the latest technology for any young '90 pound weakling' (sic) who was looking to build muscles and avoid having sand kicked in his face at the beach. It was what Charles Atlas used to achieve his dynamic Grecian form and win the Mr World competition as the worlds' strongest looking man.

My friend and I used to try to stretch the plastic coated strap of the Bullworker out to the maximum limit in one huge breath and prove our superhuman abilities thus excluding us instantly from ever needing to put in strenuous hours building huge red muscle tissue. A couple of pushes and pulls was enough, we thought, for the day and we would retire back to the TV for the rest of the afternoon. I Dream of Genie, Hogan's Heroes, Gilligan's Island, Gigantor (featuring Dr Elephant), Prince Planet, FireballXL5, Marine Boy, Astro Boy (again featuring Dr Elephant), The Avengers (Steed and Emma Peel version please), The Banana Splits (featuring the Thomson Twins in the letter box; Tra la la boomdeeyay), The Jetsons and The Road Runner etc.

What could possibly be better? Working out on a Bullworker? I don't think so! Not with Cheezels and creaming soda available to accompany the viewing of our latest and most absorbing visual entertainment technology since Shakespeare's plays in the Old Stafford.

Yeh, some girls looked at muscles but some girls looked at faces and listened to voices. The Bullworker was very quickly obsolete when chemical bulk building powders became popular and you could just take some powder in milk, lie on the couch and GROW!

Of course eventually the dark green Bullworker reclined casually against an unused corner as an ornamental curio or trophy, gathered dust and only hinted faintly that it was ever used by the owner to produce any outstanding muscular results.

Last time I heard, the muscle-building contraption had survived nine family moves, lost its tension through some hydraulic failure and was now working as a substitute leg for a small card table. Fame is etched in ice and then the sun comes up. Hence, the gradual decline of the Bullworker.

The random collection of items in my drawer was not on purpose. The drawer just happened to be a convenient place to store things that may have a future use and to keep them out of the public eye where they would not look like clutter in an unkempt house hold. Some collectors are more purposeful. There are houses and sheds and barns all over the world containing strange and bizarre collections of toys and dolls and clothes and model trains and smurfs and action figures. The recent infatuation with retro clothing and items from any era in the past are there for a reason; to recreate memories.

"Oh, my gran used to have one of those in her house," sighs my wife and she is instantly transported back to that special childhood moment. It is enough incentive for her to buy it just to keep the memory alive. She wants her granddaughter to have similar nostalgic memories and will relay her own connection with the cute kewpie doll. One day in the not too distant future her granddaughter may say the same thing. A connection of memories over five generations just from a cute doll made in the 1940's.

Every avid collector knows the story of where their pieces came from and how much they paid for it. They are loath to sell any crucial pieces lest their fond accumulated memories go with it. They put too much value on the memory and not on the item itself, then it is beyond sale and, after your collective passing, will be handed down to a family member who may be sick of the sight of it and realise $5000 instantly. The original bond between the collector and the collected grows with each intimate meeting and eventually it shepherds them gracefully to the grave. Should we let it go and just keep it as a memory? It could be worth a lot of money in today's collectible market, but is that the reason you have it in your collection or is it purely because you have an emotional attachment to that item and no amount of cash is going to release it from your grasp? Some things hold potent memories for life.

Does it give you pleasure? Does it give you status? Does it make you a more interesting person? Does it give you something to talk about or are you just wanting to share a fond memory with someone whom you hope may think differently of you because you possess this amazing unsaleable relic from the 50's? I am thinking this as I slide the drawer closed and my eyes cast down.

Under the drawer are two innocuous brown cupboard doors. I sort of know what's in there without even opening it based purely on my memory of that cupboard when I loaded it with things I wasn't ruthless enough to throw away. More memories, it's like I'm trying to capture the past as it drifts slowly from the present. There are folders of poems and songs and letters and stories that I wrote in the distant past when I was perhaps more naïve, cockier and more inclined to taking risks. There are also books stashed in there, some I've never read, some are old and valuable and some are signed by the author. In this cupboard and the surrounding boxes in the room and the bookshelf are literally hundreds of books all containing someone's memory but I try harder to recall the contents of the cupboard without opening it, like a mental training exercise trying to visualise trinkets that had not been used or looked at or handled in maybe fifteen or twenty years. My curiosity gets the better of me and I swing both doors open.

As I suspected, the dusty fake leather folder bulging to eight inches thick contains captured memories in writing from about 1972.

The folder used to belong to my father and when I had first opened it, it contained receipts from when he was a clerk in Sydney and maybe a payslip revealing a little more about his 'pre-elite forces' past but I have since managed to fill it with uncountable imaginative stories; perhaps to counteract a slimly funded financial upbringing. Another three ringed binder in the cupboard has handwritten songs and bits of my half written music which I never really considered again. Forgotten sons? Oops, I meant 'songs'. Were these the ones I was supposed to throw out so I could move on with my song-writing and forget the past? Maybe? Another red vinyl folder I had recycled from a disused students' desk has all my sons' writing in it. I had shown it to him and his fiancé on their recent visit and they read through some of the early 'Zaaz and Azza' stories and she laughed hysterically. He couldn't help but agree with her and tried through inebriated laughter to explain what he actually meant in his innocently cryptic teenage writings. The flow of words was quite clever really even if I look at it from a fellow authors' view and not with a paternal bias. He is already an imaginative and creative storyteller. He created the language of 'Shinken'! You will read the books!

Then they gave the folder back to me for safe keeping. He didn't really want to take it with him but he also didn't want me to destroy it. It is something he will eventually catch up with and he may ponder his own childhood literary iterations and maybe find his own 'drawer of memories' that has suddenly crept up on him.

Also in the cupboard is a complete course of Russian Language on cd accompanied by three books of translations of everyday conversations, 'spacibar'. The oddest collection of items has been thrown together in this space. A silverish tea strainer which used to belong to someone's grandmother is sitting inside a cut glass bowl which looks like Irish Glass and could have belonged to my grandmother Gilligan?

There are African finger drums and a wooden percussion stick which makes a 'clock' sound when you hit it. There is a random stack of books bought cheap at an op-shop or garage sale and a SKETCH-A-GRAPH Mk2. What are they all doing in my cupboard?

What else could I possibly use this space for? I try to imagine a more practical use for this abandoned square metre of my life but whatever I think of seems banal and boring compared to this eclectic collection of cupboard mates. I decide to leave them in their dark space together directly underneath the drawer of memories until the next time someone opens the door.

It seems the drawer has infected the cupboard and the infection is slowly spreading outward into the other rarely occupied storage spaces in the room; other cupboards and shelves become visible also cluttered with useless stowed items. Things that were put there so the person storing them would never have to think of them again and they would patiently remain forgotten. One day they would be somewhere else. Right now they are within reach of my hand.

Out of pure morbid and compunctious habit I pull an old blue book from the pile in the cupboard and look at the title. 'The World's Thousand Best Short Stories'. The blue cover card inside has stiffened over the years and the first page is foxed badly. The Words 'XIII RUSSIAN, Etc.' are printed at the top and the next page. It has a beautifully handwritten inscription, 'H.J. Pratten, State School, Oakfield.' The next page has an oval cameo shaped engraving of Edgar Allen Poe. The usual framed title page is next with the complete name of the book and a list of eminent international critics who helped select the thousand best stories.

It is published in London by the Educational Book Company Limited but there is no date. It is obviously timeless enough to escape dating.

Then I realise it is only volumes 13&14 of a much larger

compendium and that there aren't a thousand stories in this book, there are only 83. This volume covers Russian story tellers from Eugene N.Chirikov (b1864) to Nicolai Teleshov. It includes Skitalitz (the writing name of A. Petrov born 1868), Maxim Gorky (also born 1868) and Michail P. Artsibashev (1878-1926) to name a few.

This still didn't give me a reference point for the publishing date but I was starting to piece together a theme. Most of the authors' birthdates are given but not their death date which means they were still alive when this book was published, maybe late 18oo's? More like early 1900's I think, after the authors had been chewed over and translated for a few years by the literati of the time. The stories were varied and topical of Russian life in the late 1800's.

There were titles like 'Twenty-Six Men and a Girl', 'Laughter', 'The Clump of Lilac' 'Love is Stronger than Death' and 'Faust' in the Russian section. Not all the stories were by Russian authors though. The next forty were American and contained authors such as Poe (The Fall of the House of Usher, The Oval Portrait and The Tell-tale Heart to name a few of the eleven listed), Rip Van Winkle by Washington Irving, Jenks's Whiskers by Solomon F. Smith and various short stories by Nathaniel Hawthorne. Did anyone remember these stories or these authors? 'My Double and How He Undid Me' by Edward Everett Hale was some ten pages long in a book of 759 pages.

These were the best stories ever told according to the International Board of Eminent Critics headed by Sir William Robertson Nicoll, LL.D and edited by Sir J.A. Hammerton and here it was in my hand. A book of memories and incredible literary pieces had been lolling idly around in the cupboard below the drawer of memories. I'm tempted to keep this one out of the cupboard and read some snippets for inspiration.

Maybe I'll stumble across a story about memories or perhaps they are all a result of indomitable authors wanting to write down their memories so they may never be lost. I'll start with Rip Van Winkle and graze through the rest until I come upon a reference to memory and then I will perhaps purloin it for my own purposes, once again continuing the lost memories of the drawer. I place it near the flowers and the sea balls and the coin and the post cards on my desk.

It is a beautiful sunny winter Sunday afternoon as I'm writing this.

A guest arrives outside the study, she hears a song on the radio and I hear her say to my wife, "I'm trying to think of what phase in my life this song conjures in my head. It reminds me of some place I was when I was younger and what I was doing at that time." The song is 'Love Grows Where My Rosemary Goes' by Edison Lighthouse; another distant memory; sparked by a song this time and not by an inanimate object or a book.

Music conjures the sweetest memories, nostalgic and sentimental, all at once creating a feeling similar to what you experienced all those years ago when you heard it on top forty radio seventeen thousand times; but while it is welcome and puts a smile on your face, it is fleeting and fades quickly; much the same as the 1000 best stories ever told. Music without a pleasant thought is just music; but music written with emotion resonates in the coldest soul of humanity. The ear candy (Michael Donnelly) or the 'ear worm' as industry aficionados have coined it, is the magic connection to the soul and the nostalgic reminder of naivety and innocence which we all frivolously ignored as children. It permeates the melancholy within and draws memories like poison being sucked from a wound. But what a sweet proclamation a song can be...; lamenting, comforting, energizing, romantic or dancy.

I think of the cassette tapes in the drawer of memories; Boz Scaggs and The Big Chill Soundtrack. These songs still have powerful memories for me and where I was at the time. We were driving around Brisbane in cars, probably quite drunk or inebriated in some sense, listening to Boz and mispronouncing the lyrics. Later we would watch contemporary feel-good films with prospective girlfriends in intimate situations while enjoying the Big Chill's era- defining soundtrack. Music creates the most poignant moments in anyone's' psyche. Do you remember the first time you heard Van Morrison's 'Wavelength'?

Try to name all the music you've heard in your life-time even if you are only 18! You've probably heard some of your parents' music, your grandparents' music and believe it or not your great grandparents and great, great grandparents' music. Think of the Rolling Stones and we are already into 'Great Grandparent Hood'. Before that there was Elvis Presley, Roy Orbison, Bill Hailey, Duke Ellington, Django Reinhardt, Sonny Terry and Brownie McGee, The Beatles, The Everly Brothers, Neil Sedaka, Isaac Hayes, Ray Charles, Frank Sinatra, Fats Domino, Count Basie, The Crickets, Thelonius Monk, Miles Davis. Need I say more? Actually I will anyway just for your viewing and reminiscent listening pleasure. Dave Brubeck Quartet (Time Out), Marty Robbins (Gunfighter Ballads and Trail Songs), Ella Fitzgerald (Sings the Gershwin Songbook) Sarah Vaughan (Sarah Vaughan at Mister Kelly's) Jack Elliot (Jack takes The Floor), Billy Holliday (Lady in Satin), Tito Puente and His Orchestra (Dance Mania, Vol.1), Little Richard (Here's Little Richard),Machito (Kenya), Sabu (Palo Congo), Louis Prima (The Wildest), The Louvin Brothers (Tragic Songs Of Life).

All these songs were hits pre- Rolling 'Grandparent' Stones, during the years when Castro becomes Cuba's President, Hawaii becomes the fiftieth state of the USA, Hitler is officially declared dead, the first satellite is launched and the Hula Hoop was invented. If you remember any of these things then you are indefatigably connected to all the memories of the past and may even be the conduit by which these memories will be perpetuated into the future whether they become truth, legend or myth in twenty, thirty or a hundred years' time.

You are indubitably connected through the centuries of music because someone wanted to record it. Even recreations from the distant past were recorded on paper because Mozart or Beethoven or Stravinsky or Vivaldi wanted some future generation to share their beautiful memory of the music they created. Orchestral arrangements, Operas, music charts, Pianolas, music hall performances, vinyl records, cassette tapes, CDs, MP3s, USB's, Bluetooth downloads, I-tunes, You Tube and Spotify can all give you a taste of what influence music has had on the minds of modern men. Music is the highest of the seven liberal arts and above all else leaves a remarkably indelible memory on the medulla oblongata of every person alive on the planet. 'Some dance to remember, some dance to forget'; and yet here I hold the cassette tapes in my hand which literally transported me instantly into the musical world of pre-CD memory.

I do still have a cassette player which works but the tapes have deteriorated somewhat leaving the sound quality dubious and varying in speed. Another obsolete technology destined to take up space in a land fill. Some may be collected for posterity in a museum or for sale as decorative reminders of the past. Now the dumps of the world are filling with hard non-biodegradable plastic tapes alongside the bean stringers and Bullworkers. How long will it take to break down? I suppose CDs will eventually join the pile along with telephones, both mobile and handset versions, children's toys, printers and printer cartridges, computers, both laptop and desktop types, biros, Bic lighters, plastic storage tubs, tools, laminated posters, old lamps, discarded keyboards etc. The list of unwanted unrecyclable plastic items is infinite. We obviously weren't thinking of the end result when we made them. The focus was money and sales and the latest new labour saving device and the most fashionable 'keep up with the Joneses' lifestyle. No one thought about the end result, the cradle to grave mentality meant that you would have to dispose of the end product. The manufacturer took no responsibility for the ethical disposal of those items. Think how much it costs to dispose of a fridge or a foam mattress at your local tip; a lot more than you thought. Cradle to Cradle is the answer.

You have to pay the council to take away your rubbish and your poo and your green waste but isn't it time manufacturers were made responsible for the cassette tapes and the bean stringers and all the other outdated technology drifting through our environment for the next hundred or more years. They might be inspired to think of manufacturing environmentally friendly bio-degradable products when they are faced with a hefty bill for disposal of 'non-friendly products'. Surely we have evolved enough as intelligent humans to consider the future generations who will take guardianship of spaceship earth. What will they think of us? Is it true that every generation blames the previous one for the mistakes they made and the state of the planet? I believe the next generations will be a lot more sensitive to these issues and that the planet is in good hands. Teach your children well.

The drawer and the cupboard have suddenly appeared to me as a warning. The unnecessary accumulation of 'stuff', as I like to refer to it, is not the problem really. It is the initial purchase of the 'stuff' which I had no second thought about. Is it possible to buy everything we need with the conscience that will allow all that 'stuff' to be a 'cradle to cradle' product and not a 'cradle to grave' product? Will it have a natural attrition back into the earth or will it be hanging around for another thousand years leaking petro-chemical gases into our food crops? Now I'm tempted to go through all the items in the drawer and see if I can answer yes or no to this question. The flower could easily last another 100 years, and the coin, but the sea balls can happily deteriorate back into the earth without too much impact. The rusty staples? Maybe. The wooden chalk board compass? Yes.

The photos and the protractor and the milky ruler may have to be burnt or smashed in order to be reabsorbed into the ether. The scissors, screwdriver and bulldog clips may eventually find their way into a fossilized version of their original ore and may become useful again. It's just the plastics that worry me.

Bakelite, the original plastic from the early 1900's is still around but I have noticed the pieces are beginning to chalk up when you touch them. A fine dust that rubs off under your fingers but it will be a long time before those tiny particles are welcomely absorbed back into the earth. Oil based products are on their way out and it would be ironic to think that if we dumped all the useless plastic in one remote uninhabited location somewhere that a million years from now humans could again mine it as we had done with ancient fossilized forests and dinosaur blubber. How different would it be? Would the finely tuned future intellects have not forgotten the mistakes of previous generations and instead set up a memorial to human stupidity so that all could remember not to do this again. Oh wait, they tried to do that with politics and war and poverty and; I don't think history has taught us much about waste or stupidity. China is now filled with rubbish from around the world.

Yes, we are the disposable society. I have thoughtfully created a table of items from the many disposable items we have been lured to perpetuate indefinitely through wanting to be seen with the latest technology and thus be considered an advanced global citizen. Many of these we have to dispose of a lot quicker than we ever used to. Where does it all go?

Remember the rusting car hulks mostly made of steel in your Hillbilly neighbour's yard? Remember cloth nappies hanging on every wash line for miles? Glass milk bottles and wax paper bread wrappers were designed based on the technology of the time. Cigarette lighters, which are becoming a slowly obsolete necessity in the average household, were a lifetime thing which you filled when it became empty and you replaced the flint.

Everyone repaired their own bikes rather than dumping them when the brake pads wore out or the tire went flat. Here's the list!

Comparative table of *Necessary* items for the modern home.

Item	Purpose	Disposal (*Now*)	Disposal (*Then*)	Recyclability (*Now*)	(*Then*)
Car	Convenient and time saving travel.	3-5 years	10-lifetime	X Plastic	$ Steel
TV	Entertainment beyond the radio and cards. Babysitting.	5-10 years?	Til it really died from being hit. They were expensive!	X	Wood & Glass
Nappies	Convenient poo catchers for babies.	It's in the dump in in less than a week!	Simply wash and reuse over and over.	X	Cotton
Cigarette Lighters	The secret of fire without burning a pine forest of matches.	A couple of weeks, a month?	Kept and reused, handed down heirloom.	X	Rarely discarded, no plastic.
Milk Bottles	Allow people the dignity of consuming milk without having to squeeze a cow's teat.	Instant		OK	Glass

Item	Purpose	Disposal (*Now*)	Disposal (*Then*)	Recyclability	
				(*Now*)	(*Then*)
Shoes	Allow humans to look semi-dignified at family events such as weddings, prevent hookworm.	A couple of years if they're tough or one year if you are a growing child.	Hand me downs, well made, and reheeled. Employed cobblers.	?	Leather, rubber, nails?
Phone	Annoy people	3 months?	Lifetime piece	X	X

Now make your own list of items and see which ones are recyclable and which ones are obsolete. Also see how hard it is to throw away something that contains fond memories and see how full your drawer still is when you decide what you are going to throw and what you are going to keep.

Alas, some people are not that sentimental and will easily be able to empty the drawer in one fell swoop. It doesn't mean they've thrown the memory away, just the physical stimulus for that memory. No matter how hard they try they will never be able to erase it. At some point in the future, perhaps during a social conversation, the stimulus will be mentioned and they are instantly back in that moment when it was tossed and for a brief second, the thread that connected them returns like an inescapable snapshot of their past. The persistence of memory.

How much are you willing to remember? Or forget?

GOLDY 8

Loretta

It was the strategically positioned Texan hat that caught my attention. Underneath it was a shock of blonde curls and a beaming mouthful of pearly whites. No makeup for this cowgirl. Her hazel-brown eyes shone with the mischief that can only result from being in the great outdoors astride a frisky stallion. Genuine R.M. Williams riding boots skipped to the bar and she ordered a cold beer off the tap. Al obliged and said, "There ya go ma'am" in true country speak. She sculled it down with practiced finesse, licked her lips and ordered another. I played 'Mamas don't let your babies grow up to be cowboys' and she turned to me with a knowing look and let out a huge 'Yeeha!'

"C'mon boy, let er rip," she said raising her beer to me "How about some Hank Williams?"

I obliged by playing 'Get that marryin outta ya head, I'll be a bachelor for life.' She was enamoured enough with my country repertoire to saunter on over and splay her elbows on the piano splashing beer on to poor Kawai with reckless abandon.

She slapped the laminated top several times as I finished the song and said "You're pretty good man; know any Loretta Lynn songs?" I thanked her and wanted to say 'no fuck off I don't play country' but I'd already played two and she was placing a twenty in my tip jar. I played 'Coal Miner's Daughter' and she nearly teared up singing along with the chorus. Despite her garrulous exterior I sensed a deeper tortured soul who had run away from home to escape the big city and all its sins.

"Where you from cowgirl?" I asked to change the sad country mood that had washed over her.

"I'm from all over and nowhere," she replied seeming to

have used that line before and finishing her beer. There was a slight American twang to her vowels that gave her away. "My daddy was a coalminer."

"Oooh, mysterious Loretta," I replied while starting up a rendition of 'Lord it's hard to be Humble'.

"Somewhere in the mid-west I imagine," I asked looking up from the keyboard for a reaction.

"Nope, more west than that; Californ-I-A if you must know. Buy you a beer sonny?" she asked as she headed to the bar again starting to appear a bit pissy.

"No thanks ma'am, not while I'm playing, gotta visit the bathroom anyway" I said and stood to walk to the stinkiest loo in history.

My ablution was brief and low-lit as a result of several bulbs blown out during the recent floods through the roof. The one good light over the sink meant my face wasn't illuminated in the mirror and I thought the guy standing in front me projected a decent silhouette until one of the bulbs flashed to life and I realised I was looking at a poster of the upcoming Saturday night act known as 'The Rogue'. He played blues guitar and was devastatingly young and handsome and I hoped at least that he had a bad attitude to compensate for all his other talents but as I moved to the left I saw the unfortunate visage of a thirteenth century monk who could have starred in 'The Name of the Rose'. I picked at the cold sore scabs under my nose and one began to bleed so I splashed it with water hoping I would suddenly appear like a recently remodelled Hollywood hipster but only succeeded in creating a bloody flow that would rival the Yangtze River dam in flood.

A punter walked in to piss and eyed me suspiciously as I tried to stem the flow with Norman Gunston style toilet paper squares. I kept imagining Loretta storming through the door to ride me like a knackered bull on the slippery toilet floor but it was just wishful thinking.

I re-emerged into the dimly lit bar and noticed Loretta side-saddle on the piano stool tinkering with the Kawai. She noticed the blood on my face immediately and then pointed at the punter who had just relieved himself and said, "Did he do that to you?" Before I could say no she had rounded the piano and grabbed the poor unsuspecting pisser by the collar and dragged him to the floor face down grabbing his legs up behind him like he was hog-tied. With her knee firmly placed in his back he yelled like a high-pitched castrato and Al was there in an instant.

"What's going on here miss?" he asked not so calmly.

"This punk bloodied up your piano player, look at him." Al looked at my bleeding face for an explanation and I began to say that it wasn't him, it was…" and promptly fell to the floor, passed out from blood loss as was my peculiar condition called avascular vago which I had experienced on several occasions after donating blood.

Apparently, I returned to consciousness within 60 seconds and was told that Loretta had indeed unleashed a most un-ladylike beating on the poor unsuspecting teenager who was on a first date with his new boyfriend. Al had trouble dismantling the affray and called the police and ambulance who walked in as I was sitting up on the alcohol-stained carpet trying to figure out who I was and how I got there. Loretta was cradling my head and stroking me like a new born puppy that's been run over by a tractor. I was in heaven looking into the hazel brown eyes of the coal miner's daughter when a fat policeman pushed her aside assisted by a butch ambo. They checked me over shining lights into my eyes and quickly realised the source of my fainting, stemming it with a quick dab of Vaseline. I stood unsteadily and sat at the piano as Loretta looked anxiously on.

Al pointed the ambo at the poor victim still writhing on the floor who was now in fact hog-tied by his own tie and beginning to choke himself.

Loretta snarled at him as they carried him out to the

ambulance accompanied by his shocked doting date and turned to me and said sympathetically, "You alright fella?" as though she was talking to her horse. I couldn't lie, "I'm fine thanks Loretta, just a little blood loss, that's all."

She stroked my forehead and I found Kawai's ever receptive ivories with my fingers and began to play 'Everything will be alright tonight', not wanting to tell the truth and spoil the affection she was showing me. Al eyed me suspiciously as he cleaned glasses. The policeman returned promptly and asked if I wished to press charges. "No, I think he's learnt his lesson," I said looking at Loretta and smiling. "Don't mess with a cowgirls' cowboy." Loretta smiled and ordered fresh beers. Mine sat getting stale on the piano as I played suicidally sad country songs and she proceeded to mutate into an ornery cowgirl from nowhere.

I do remember being thrown over her shoulder and escorted back to my apartment where she proceeded to take off her stinky boots and socks, asked me to remove her painted on jeans with much difficulty and collapse in my bed as though she owned it. All I could do was stand and watch my saviour sleep as only a drunken cowgirl could; and she snored louder than a stampede until dawn.

Music is the champion of all arts, moving hearts and feet,
Telling the stories of the brash and the meek,
Soothing your soul with rhythms and rhyme,
Elevating your mind beyond space and time;

Try to pick it up or capture its' charms
And you may find a dancing partner in your arms;
It doesn't pay much and it costs so much less
But may cause the enthusiasts to don a special dress;

It occupies the deepest parts of your mind,
Never meant to be forgotten, played by artists sublime;
What would life be without a melodic tune
When relaxing in the late winter afternoon;

I can't imagine a day when no-one wants to sing along,
to that magical, mystical, musical song; Viva Musica

GOLDY 9

Heavenly Helen

It was a quiet night with the usual sad faces occupying their favourite positions around the bar. Ten Ton Tessie was downing Doritos and rum beside her best friend Derek the Vegetarian who was drinking chardonnay. The only inkling I had that someone had walked through the swing doors was when they swung quietly back into place as she padded across the floor like a Jedi on the moons of Naboo. I was finishing a 'Go Betweens' song as the little blonde bob bobbed to the bar and ordered a Cosmopolitan. Al screwed his face up like a taxi driver who doesn't know where to go and she obliged him by suggesting cranberry juice and vodka which he didn't have so eventually she settled for a screwdriver and looked around the room like a lost kitten.

Once I had eye contact she smiled playfully and I felt I had found one of my own purely through psychic connection and the fact she was shorter than me but extremely well stacked. She had the cheekiest bedroom eyes on the planet and proceeded to approach me as I shuffled uncomfortably through the David Bowie song 'Sorrow'.

"Gidday, how ya doin?" she said with a somewhat unexpected Aussie twang. Her voice was tempered with sexuality and matter-of-factness and I smiled for the first time in years like I had met a soul mate worthy of a conversation. I stopped playing and reached over to introduce myself and shake her hand which was warm, tiny and soft. She looked me square in the eyes as she said her name was Helen.

"What a coincidence? Both our names end in 'en'; I'm Stephen." She giggled like an elf and smiled a bit wider revealing her generously proportioned teeth; truly lovely.

Usually the punters pepper me with requests but she was happy for me to finish my version of Sting's 'If you love somebody' and sip her screwdriver while I sang at her. Her cool blue eyes studied me with flippant intentions; she finished her drink and asked directions to the ladies. I pointed to the right keeping my left hand firmly pressed on the E minor. I watched her tiny feet taking tiny steps in her very sexy shoes towards the 'Ladies' and hoped Al had renewed the toilet paper after the cat fight in there the night before. I saw the opportunity to freshen up in my personal Green Room and dashed to the 'Gentleman's' otherwise known by the locals as 'Le Pissoir'.

Disgusted with my cheap haircut and withered face I splashed water over my whole head and took a deep breath but I came up looking like a drowned rat sporting unsightly ear and nose hairs. I futilely attempted to pluck them out and after much pain and sneezing winked at the man in the mirror assuring him he was more dapper than the fella who'd walked in there five minutes ago. Confidence was everything at this point so I relieved myself, washed my hands and stood taller as I walked back to the piano.

She wasn't there. I waited, playing a few Donald Fagen tunes and then began to worry that she had left. I looked at Al and he signalled to the 'Ladies' as if to say she was still in there. He had also been keeping a keen eye on her and raised his hands as if to say, 'I don't know'. I played Michael Franks and Frank Zappa and then Frank Sinatra but she didn't appear. I became concerned for my little flirty Helen and said to Al, "Hey you wanna check and see if she's alright."

"You check, I'm busy." He was and there were no other women in the bar who I could ask to check on my lovely Helen.

Cautiously I pushed the 'Ladies' door opened and called, "Anyone in there?" I'd never been in this hallowed place before and walked to the sinks calling again, "Hello? Helen?"

"In here" cooed the muffled voice from the furthest cubicle. "I need some toilet paper," came the sheepish reply.

"Ok," I panicked and searched each cubicle realising that Al had not replaced the decorations used in last nights' bitch-fight toilet extravaganza. Fortunately there were two paper towelets left in the dispenser and I carefully reached under the door and handed them to her only to be confronted with the foulest stench I had ever had the misfortune to pass through my nostrils. I gagged and held my nose thinking that not even my dog had produced such a smell even after eating its own left over vomit. It smelled like she had been feeding in a Mumbai fish market after bathing in the Luggage Point sewage treatment plant, but worse. She thanked me and I tippy-toed to the door hoping not to permanently impregnate my cheap suit with the 'Dr Evil' of stinks but a feint after-smell of peanut paste lingered in the air and helped me mentally make it back to the door. I felt like the Bear Grylls of toilet adventurers. Outside I gladly breathed in the stale smoky air of the bar and wiped myself down before approaching poor little Kawai. I played 'Don't Take Me Alive' by Steely Dan and some Japanese tourists walked in and stood close to the piano suddenly noticing the stench attached to me. They all screwed their noses up and ordered Saki.

Helen suddenly teetered over to them and joined in the Saki swilling festivities. Apparently, she was their tour guide and being slightly taller than them and having blonde hair, commanded an audience with her fluent Japanese, saying that the smell was usual for an Australian lounge bar because of the cheap food and perspiration of the hard-working Aussies. They all laughed and sculled their Saki, which Al, luckily, had been given by his mother who frequented Japan to complete her Black Belt in Origami and Kendo.

I don't know how I knew what Helen was saying to them but she looked sideways at me and winked and I knew I would forgive her for the most mind numbing indelible memory I'd ever had implanted in my olfactory senses. Nothing could compare to the stink of Helen. I knew she had laid herself bare and I could finally relax into a conversation with her knowing I would never mention it again in our lifetime.

At her tour group's request I played 'Jimi Hendrix', 'The New York Dolls' and 'Rou Reed' while all the time keeping my eyes firmly attached to Helen's through the smoky noise of naughty Japanese business men away from home and whooping it up in a sleazy piano bar with a beautiful young blonde Aussie girr. Eventually they were singing like it was a karaoke bar and using empty stubbies for mics but to their credit they knew lots of songs and one of them confessed to me that he learnt English by singing in a karaoke bar; he then proceeded clumsily to try to polish Kawai's glossed mahogany finish with a splash of Suntory to christen our musical union... Then he said, "Oh? Kawai? Japanese? Good."

Helen herded the tourists towards the exit before midnight like an Aussie cattle dog on a flock of sheep in New Zealand. She thanked me and Al for our kind hospitality and I sensed that she would return. Al was reluctant to see them go and offered takeaways but they noisily made their way on to the street as I sat at the bar for a welcome break.

"Wow, she's a little dynamo," said Al counting his exorbitant Thursday night takings with his tongue hanging out the side of his mouth helping him count.

"Let me tell you a little story about Heavenly Helen Al, she has the most potent..."

"Most potent what?" She was right there beaming cheekily at me before I delivered the real punchline to Al. Al looked over his shoulder at me but didn't ask.

"The most potent pulchritudinous perky peepers I've ever peered into in my previous years."

She smiled widely and her eyes glowed with other worldly knowing. "Is that a tongue twister?" she asked naively and giggled. "It could be?" I replied cryptically.

She ordered a beer and said in her slightly Western Queensland tinged brogue, "So what are we gonna do now eh?"

The thought of a return to her stench wasn't enough to deter me; being a lonely male I couldn't resist the charms of a beautiful woman no matter how she smelled.

Al looked up at me as if to say, 'Here we go again?!'

As we walked from the bar quite close, she turned to look up at me and said,

"Did you smell that disgusting smell in the toilets before? God, that woman who walked out as I arrived should have her bowels checked." I realised in that moment that the peanut paste smell which assisted me to the door of the Ladies was in fact Helens 'odour de toilette' and that I had inadvertently walked in on the aftermath of Ten Ton Tessie's weekly Mexican-fuelled unloading... mmmm?

EARTH MAGGOTS

A recent conversation with a close friend sparked off some horrific realizations about the world we live in in 2023. I think we had both reached an age where we could qualify as 'old farts' and therefore had gained some understanding of the way 'things' work in the world regardless of the fact that some 'things' seem to be repeated despite the universal realization that those things were inherently stupid to begin with. Over a few drinks we began to compile a list of things that could be changed to improve the world in general for the benefit of the majority instead of the unjustly wealthy minority. We agreed that humans are more like maggots crawling over each other to get to the next meal.

In Buddhism, the ultimate goal is to reach Nirvana which is described as a place where you have rid yourself of 'want'. Unfortunately this is quite difficult for most humans as people always 'want' more than they have even if they have billions of dollars. One of the main culprits in creating 'want' is fashion. Now don't get me wrong; I don't think everyone should be wearing a communist provided outfit of hard wearing work clothes (although it would solve some world-wide waste problems). I do appreciate fashion as a way to make you feel good about yourself, look better than being naked and to be different and individual.

My issue is with the waste involved. Fashion this spring becomes land fill by summer, new styles come out each season and it is embarrassing if you have to wear the same clothes but there is a limit to recycling and while some fashion guru in the middle of Europe has decided that maroon and silk is the new black, everyone rushes like hungry maggots to get the latest. Of course not everyone is concerned with impressing people with their clothes and most men will have a suit they keep for weddings, funerals and court appearances.

Op shops and vintage clothing fairs have become a great way to buy used clothing cheaply and to recycle but on a global scale, there are literally thousands of tonnes a year which goes to landfill.

The peer pressure on teenage girls to wear the latest fashion has resulted in some embarrassing visuals especially with the advent of the Brazilian v string and the all important active wear outfits which are hardly ever used for gym or physical activity. If you thought men in cycling lycra was embarrassing you won't have to look far to see a fashion faux pas being worn by a majority of women who have been influenced by the 'latest' fashion. Men are also victims as they feel it necessary to sport an armful of meaningless tattoos, muscly arms which are wasted on every day activities, a top knot and a beard which goes with the sports cap and a twin cab ute. If you have all these things, board shorts and a surf shirt, then you are fashionable and you can 'fit in' with the rest of society. Not everyone embraces this 'modern' look but it changes very quickly.

I remember not that long ago when men with beards were thought to be untrustworthy and clean shaven meant you were honest. The army buzz cut has come back big time and now, the once scoffed at mullet has come hurtling back into fashion via the strong influence of NRL footballers. When we were at school in the seventies everyone had long hair and many had some kind of mullet. With the influence of the Brit invasion to Australia, barbers can give you a pretty good flat top to wear to your favourite British music show. Things change very quickly and it's expensive to keep up with the latest fashion; if you feel the need.

Besides being responsible for nearly 10% of global carbon emissions, the average person throws away up to 50 kilos of textile waste per year (including clothing), nearly two million tonnes of textiles waste every year and an increase of 50% expected by 2030. The throw away culture has worsened where clothes are only ever worn 7 to 10 times before being tossed.

The fashion industry is responsible for 20% of global waste water where colour and other chemicals are used in fabrics. These are energy intensive processes based on fossil fuel energy. It takes 20,000 litres of water to produce one kilogram of cotton and $500 billion is lost each year because of 'under- wearing' and failure to recycle clothes. At least 10% of micro- plastics in the ocean come from textiles and 3 million tonnes of returned clothing ended up in land fill in 2020 in the US alone. Fast fashion brands produce twice the amount of clothing today than in 2000.

What is the solution you may ask? There are probably a thousand solutions but if you are aware of the issue, you might wear your clothes more before you throw them out, recycle and donate to charity, keep a rag bag in your garage and be careful about what clothes you buy and what they are made from. Renting clothes for a special occasion has become popular too. Don't bitch to me about climate change if you are part of the problem and not part of the solution. What are you doing to make a difference?

Have you noticed how much food is wasted? Have you noticed how many cooking shows are aired daily on Australian TV? Supermarkets regularly throw out food by the skip load and the average weekly shopper throws away up to a third of their weekly grocery shop. There is an abundance of food on the planet and yet I see ads on TV asking for donations to help those less fortunate in other countries. Why can't those countries feed their own people? Shouldn't we be concentrating on the needy in our own country first? Does any of our wasted food go to help anyone else in the world or is it too costly? Most of the grain grown in the world goes to feed livestock. The US could feed 800 million people with grain that livestock eat.

Nearly 40% of world grain is being fed to livestock rather

than being consumed directly by humans (Earth Maggots). Humans require about 3.7 billion tonnes of food a year to feed everyone. We produce about 4 billion tonnes but about 1.3 billion tonnes goes to waste. Some clever Earth Maggots came up with a plan to supply enough food for two earth's worth of people without clearing any new farmland but still 270 million people could be living in famine by the end of this year. How stupid must we be that we have so much waste, an idea to fix it and yet no progress because the money should be spent elsewhere?

Unfortunately, there are some greedy Earth Maggots out there who think there are things with a higher priority than feeding everyone. Could you guess what that might be? Between China, India, USA and Brazil, enough food is produced annually to feed everyone on two planets. If Australia didn't export any of its produce, we could feed our own population, New Guinea, New Zealand, several Pacific Islands and more without batting an eyelid.

Someone recently claimed that if every Earth Maggot lived like the average Indian then we could support 30 billion people. To find out if it's true I asked some of the more affluent Earth Maggots in my neighbourhood some rather poignant questions. I'll try to paraphrase rather than directly quote what was said but in a nutshell... (To a couple who have a sign on their fence saying 'Climate Change Now!) I asked what they meant by having that sign on their fence and they passionately said that the government and council should do more towards reducing the negative influences of climate change which they stated were 'global warming and rising sea levels'. When I asked if they had seen any rise in the sea level nearby they said they hadn't but they didn't want to be inundated in their lifetime (despite the fact they lived at least a kilometre from the shore and well above sea level). I asked if they didn't mind if it happened after they died and they sort of nodded.

I asked about the two huge diesel 4x4's in the driveway

and suggested that they were using fossil fuels so weren't they contributing to the climate change? They defended themselves by saying they were going to go electric soon. I asked how they would charge the vehicles and they scoffed, saying that they have special power points installed and the electric bikes were already charging. I noted that their power would still come from mostly burning coal but they had enough solar to run the lights in their house. Once they get back from their trip to Asia and Europe they would look at buying an electric car. (Recently, electric car sales have dropped by over 41% globally.)

I noted the use of airline fuel in their trip of several plane rides over the planet and sensitive environmental landscapes that would be affected by their journey. They stopped and looked at me as though I had punched them in the face. I asked them what they are doing to prevent climate change and they said they have a recycling bin and they use magnesium in their pool instead of salt.

I overheard a woman talking at a coffee shop to her friend about how disgusting climate change was. 'How can they do that to our planet?' I couldn't help myself and butted in to their conversation. "Excuse me for over-hearing (she did have a loud voice) but who is 'they'?" She looked at me blankly and asked, "I beg your pardon?"

"When you were talking about climate change, you said, how can 'they' do that to our planet? I was just wondering who 'they' was?" Again a blank look and a sideways look at her friend who also raised her eyebrows. Then she said,

"You know, the government and those people in charge of things, why?"

My turn to look them both in the eye this time and then I said,

"Aren't we all responsible for making changes in our lifestyle so that we leave a smaller footprint for future generations?"

"Like what?" she asked amused and a bit put out by my

interruption.

"Well, you know simple things like recycling or using less air conditioning in our house and being conscious of how much water we use..." I left it hanging.

"Why should I sweat it out while all those pollie bastards are sitting in their ivory towers sucking up the air con?

No, I worked hard to get all the privileges I have and my nice car and house and I'm not willing to give it up for anyone." She was truly incensed and so was her friend. "I have a recycle bin, isn't that enough?"

"Then you are as much a part of the problem as anyone and you should stop complaining about the climate change created by 'them'. You don't really know what climate change is and if you did, and you really cared, you would make some effort to lower your footprint on this earth even if it is for our future generations."

At this point I had to stand up and walk away hoping she would never recognize me again but she called out, "So what are you doing to make a change smartarse?" I could have just kept walking but couldn't help myself.

"I'm just calling out you armchair activists hoping you'll spread the word and tell your friends what I said. Do some research before you blame 'them' for something you are responsible for." I didn't mention that I have a huge credit on my electricity bill and my wife and I use less water than a one person household. Oh, and I pick up rubbish from the beach every day. Imagine if everyone picked up three pieces a day; 78 million pieces less rubbish. What are you doing to be part of the solution?

I know, I'm an agitator, always have been, calling out the bullshit and the phonies even though I have probably been guilty myself at some time in my life. I do admit to throwing butts out the window of my car and probably other garbage and I had no second thought about it. Now that I've become a cranky old fart, I can't help calling out people who blatantly waste, refuse to pick up their dog's shit, leave their broken beach umbrella at the beach, let the wind blow their fish and chips packaging into the nearby creek and smash their empty stubbies onto the rocks below the headland where children will play the next day.

An American driving along a part of pristine wilderness was throwing his empty beer bottles out the window and his friend said, "Hey, why are you polluting this natural environment?" The driver looked at his friend as he was throwing another empty out the window and said, "They have already fucked with this environment, look at this massive piece of asphalt stretching off into the distance. His friend couldn't disagree.

But what I'm talking about here is just local and very minor compared to what is going on globally. Mining companies cover up dumping toxic waste, government departments throw away thousands of computers into landfill each year, schools are too lazy to recycle their paper (up to 1500 kilos per school per year on average) mountains of fridges, tyres and used cars, not to mention the unseen tonnes of cargo that falls off ships and is never recovered. That is just the beginning. Just excuse me for a minute while I empty my recycling bin hoping to make a difference in the world. Apparently, waste is someone else's problem.

Another of the huge polluters on the planet which somehow escapes the news is beauty packaging which includes plastic, paper, glass and metals that are improperly recycled and ultimately end up in landfill. Over 120 billion units of trash is produced by the beauty industry each year. Cosmetics is a 50 billion dollar a year industry and continuing to grow with markets opening up in previously restricted countries like China, south Asia and the Middle East. In the past, Earth Maggots made perfumes from ambergris which is a secretion of the bile duct in the intestines of sperm and pygmy whales and provides a marine-like odour. They also used secretions from the glands of civets which were farmed and kept in cages to collect the soft yellow material and dilute it into a sweet aroma.

The anal gland of the beaver creates a leathery animalistic scent and the musk deer produces glandular secretions which give off a complex earthy and woody smell.

I doubt that there are many exotic scents made this way anymore with the advent of scientific advances in scent technology. In Australia alone we splash out roughly $20 billion per year or $431 per person each month.

There is no responsible manufacturing when it comes to making people more beautiful. Funny how all the commercials show extremely young women using 'youth producing' products. The chemicals and research into these products is dubious to say the least, hyaluronic acid? Collagen plumping? Overnight results? Look younger in a week? What happened to bee venom that was so popular a few years ago? Did it fail or did they sell out of the hard to milk and cruel practice of bee venom milking where 1600 bees died to provide a younger looking face for one 23 year old?

Petrochemicals are a major ingredient in most cosmetics and so the beauty industry would want oil and petroleum mining to continue so they can sell $20 more billion next year. They also contain allergens, alpha hydroxyl acids, beta hydroxyl acids, colour additives, diethanolamine, latex, parabens and artificial beaver anus fragrance. They also use talc, mica particles and silica as fillers; iron oxides, titanium dioxide and organic dyes as pigments. There are also an abundance of emollients, surfactants, formaldehyde, methylene glycol, quaterniium15, mercury dibutyl, and phthalates. I could go on but you would end up with a chemistry degree by the end of it. There are 50,000 people in the US alone working in the cosmetics industry which is now a $429.2 billion a year global industry. The cosmetics industry is growing by at least 3% per year.

Would you sacrifice some of your beauty regimen to provide

housing for the poor or support children with terminal cancer? What could those billions of dollars be used for to make the world a better place? How much less polluted could our landfill be without the waste from cosmetic products?

Accept that you are mortal and grow old gracefully. There's a lot to be said about a healthy diet, exercise and a cheerful outlook on life.

Try to avoid the 'want' and think about others who may be less fortunate than yourself. Now go to your bathroom cabinet, look at how much you have spent on snake oils and magic unguents and throw them away. Keep only the essential medicinal products and start saving some money.

Oh by the way, if you bitch about climate change and you shower for more than 3-5 minutes, you are wasting the world's precious water, so shut up. Teenagers are mostly to blame (probably girls more than boys). The average shower time is about 8 minutes and uses 96 litres. Some people shower for a lot longer and can use between 150 to 350 litres in one shower. If they do that every day of the week it results in more than 1400 litres per week and up to 72800 litres per year. If every Australian did that we would be using 18,928,000,000,000 litres of water on the driest continent on earth. Good work you nib nob Earth Maggots! What the fuck are you doing in there for 20 mins? Wash yourself and your hair if you need to and you are still out in less than five minutes. I just rolled my eyes.

Only 3% of the water on the planet is fresh and of that 3% only 1.5 % is available for human use as the rest is inaccessible in icecaps and glaciers. Antarctica has 90% of the world's fresh water. The top five countries which have the highest volume of renewable fresh water are Brazil, Russia, USA, Canada and China. Australia is way down low on the list.

How long does your shower take? Do you let the tap run when you are brushing your teeth? (Nine litres per minute) Naughty climate change contributor you!

When we were growing up we had pets. Stray kittens lodged under our house because we lived near KFC and they were obviously dumped by someone. We tried to tame them as they hissed at us and eventually we fed them scraps and titbits left over from dinner.

They were never allowed inside the house but they would hang around the back door, explore the back yard and sleep in an old tea chest under the house. One morning they were gone. Only the mother cat remained which my brother very cleverly called 'mother'. I remember early one morning overhearing a conversation between two adults who had agreed to dump the kittens somewhere. When I found out how it was done I was horrified. (It involved a sugar bag and a creek).

Mother cat stayed with us for a while and then had another litter with a KFC stray once she was on heat. Again the kittens disappeared without a trace or an explanation from any of the adults in the house.

My uncle had dogs on his property. They loved him and all his family. They barked when a car arrived, chased vermin and ate whatever he gave them which was mostly human scraps from dinner. They lay on an old sugar bag outside the back door. Even his cat, which just appeared one day, pretended to be a dog and became a very good ratter. There was no expense involved in having a pet. Sometimes the dog would be tied up on a run with some food, water and bones for a few days while my uncle and his family was away for a long weekend but the dog would greet them loyally with a howl when they got home.

Fast forward to today and a cat or dog will cost you between $3000and $6000 in the first year of ownership. After that you will spend an average of $3218 each year for a dog. Bunnings now has two aisles for pets and their accessories and food. Australians spent $33.2billion in 2022 to keep their pets fed, healthy, groomed and accessorized. One of my friends spent $6000 in vet bills to find his French Bulldog had snorted a pea up his nose.

Almost every cafe on the Sunny Coast has accommodated pet owners to have 'Poochy' under their table and in some cases in a chair beside them. This would never have been seen twenty years ago when people left their dog tied up at home.

There are dog parks where owners will loyally pick up Poochy's shit in specially made plastic dog shit bags which then go into landfill. At the beach in the morning dogs can run free, piss where they like, drop runny poos on the sand and generally frolic like spoiled children until 9a.m. Then the humans are allowed to come to the beach and find a place that doesn't smell like piss, shit or wet dog and hope their toddlers don't trip face first into a glob of dog shit sand that was overlooked by an absent-minded dog owner.

Last Christmas I rode my bike down to the beach for a look at the ocean and was confronted by a hundred dogs and their owners celebrating a doggy Christmas which apparently had been approved by the council. There was a seat for the dogs to sit beside Santa and have their photo taken and Earth Maggots with elf costumes and ears feeding special doggy Christmas treats to the plethora of breeds which were frolicking on the sand and in the creek like it was their god-given right to be spoiled. I wondered at that moment where the Earth Maggots had come up with this ridiculous decision in their lives.

Don't get me wrong, I love dogs and most cats but this was over the top. Most people don't spend that much on their children's education. Imagine if all that money was spent on something crucial like housing for the poor or children suffering from debilitating illness or smart ways to dispose of dog shit. Yes, I know I sound cynical; that's because I am. Shut up!

A close family member is planning to take their dog on holiday to Tasmania. I reminded them that Tassie is mostly National Park and doesn't allow dogs.

They were *not* going to leave the dog in a luxurious resort kennel but decided to fly the dog from Melbourne to Launceston while her husband takes the van over on the ferry. Dogs are not allowed on the ferry. The dog will cost five hundred dollars for the flight each way and she will have to fork out her own airfare to Launceston and back on the same flight. Once they get to the National Parks they wish to explore, they will take it in turns to walk the beautiful tracks and tag team looking after the dog. They will not be able to explore the beauty of Tasmania together because of their fucking dog. Tell me what is wrong with this situation. The dog is the most important creature in this relationship. I'm rolling my eyes again.

I think I'd like to be reincarnated as one of their pets even if they only live for about 15 years because I would be more loved than any previous pet on the planet. I'm sure I would also be just as happy being stray and fed scraps where I could find them. Oh how Earth Maggots personify the thoughts of dogs to suit themselves. If only they knew that all the dog is thinking is, 'if I pull this face and turn my head, they will overfeed me and pat me on the head to encourage me to repeat this behaviour.' Pets have become a billion dollar industry to sap money from stupid Earth Maggots. I know lap dogs can be a godsend for the lonely, elderly and physically restricted but it has become exorbitantly expensive. Maybe a cheeky parrot or a budgie might be more manageable and affordable.

I asked a hypothetical question in a group of mixed age and sex. Could you grow and or kill your own food? Most had never had to think about it and nodded blank. One person said, "Now why would I do that when there's a perfectly good supermarket stacked with food down the road." He laughed as though it was a ridiculous question. Another in the group had thought a little deeper and answered that they couldn't kill anything because they were a firm believer in animal rights. I asked if she was a vegetarian and she said no. I asked if her animal rights belief extended to chickens, pigs, sheep, cows, horses, fish, crabs or snails. She saw the loophole immediately and said, "No, I couldn't kill any of those animals." I said, "So it's ok for someone else to kill for you to eat meat?" She scratched her head, rolled her eyes and said, "Now you're making me feel guilty," and walked off. Most of the group had grown some herbs or vegetables at some stage; nothing to fill the larder every week but an attempt had been made. The list of excuses ranged from 'I don't have the time' 'I couldn't be bothered' 'I don't know how to' 'it's cheaper to buy the food than spend all that money on soil and seeds and fertilizer and water'. I asked a few of them if they knew where to get fresh water or bush tucker without a tap or bottle or shop. One said rain, another said bush limes, a third said wild mushrooms. They were all band-aid answers. I told them all that I was genuinely not going to rely on any of them if some apocalyptic event prevented regular channels of food from being available.

Technology is the key. If all the internet and electricity and phones went dead, everything would stop. No fuel for the trucks to deliver food, no communication to organise an agreed system of delivery, no lighting, no water purification plant, no sewerage being treated, no refrigeration and utter chaos on deciding who gets priority of the remaining resources. It would eventually become every Earth Maggot for themselves, armed with weapons if necessary to take what they need by pure force. There would be little civil communication for fair barter and those with a drinkable water source and stores of food become targets who will need to defend their preciously guarded and cleverly collected supplies.

Tribal war becomes a reality. Those who assist in protecting the precious food, get to share the spoils. As more people arrive to plunder what they think is rightfully theirs, they realize that the wealthy farmer or landowner who can still grow his own food becomes very powerful indeed and his popularity grows when people volunteer to assist him for just food, water and shelter. But desperation can lead Earth Maggots to do rash things and with little thought they can become enraged and lash out, wanting to kill the farmer and take it for themselves. Then others follow suit and usually the fittest survive although I'd like to think the intelligent know too, how to survive. The most powerful with the biggest stick are not always a match for a determined group of intellectuals with a well laid plan. And thus, social liberalism is born and the fascist dictator is defeated.

Let's hope the smarter of the Earth Maggots has a plan that will look after everyone, engage everyone in a positive search for what is needed to survive. What things have become useless in this society sit idle and their value is reduced to zero. Cars, video games, phones, TV's, computers are all as useful as a post-war bean stringer sitting in the second drawer of the kitchen. Earth Maggots look at their now silent devices sitting amongst the furniture in their house and have fond memories of what it was like to watch TV or chat with family on social media sites or look for pictures of drowned cats on You Tube. Without keyboards people would have to start writing by hand again but what would they write? Not shopping lists or letters because there is no shop and no mail delivery but maybe they'll write stories about the good old days when technology enabled them to live like kings and not be spied on by anyone...?

Now the glass on the laptop is good for starting fires with the help of the sun. There is not enough dry wood but we should gather some anyway so we have a supply when the winter comes and to cook. (I'm sure Scotland was deforested at one point because it was so fucking cold they took every bit of timber they could find.)

The back yard salt water pool can be used for water if the salt is boiled off, then the salt can be used for other purposes until of course, the water becomes more rainwater than salt and it may run out quickly unless it rains and all the drains are diverted to tanks and the pool. 'Shut up, you know what I mean bitchez'. No one wants to swim in the water supply but they use the water sparingly to wash and try to maintain a reasonable level of hygiene. Soap is running out but there has to be a plant based alternative. Maybe wash in the salty ocean or a nearby stream with some sudsy eucalyptus leaves and, oh yeah, Sandy Robbins is a slut. No but yeah but no! Shut up; you are still reading this trash you nib nob. Have a cup of tea and come back for the next rave. Play my favourite music in the break while I go and have a ..../+*poo^&$#@===. Alright, you're back then, listen up...

Cars are abandoned in the streets, shopping centres, train stations, garages and outside philandering maggot's homes. For weeks, Earth Maggots tried to push their cars from the train station or shopping centre towards home after the electronics failed and they ran out of some type of combustible petroleum and then realized half way home the absolute valuelessness of the vehicle now that there was no electricity to pump fuel out of big underground reservoirs in all the petrol stations in Australia. Instead of abandoning their cars they rallied their close neighbours and friends to look after each other's vehicles until they could figure out a way of getting the fuel out of those giant underground reservoirs without blowing anyone up. Of course, the owners of the underground petroleum tanks had to put security on their extremely valuable assets to prevent random raids from scientifically ignorant Earth Maggots. The sudden realization that all that fuel was still there underground sparked a kind of 'Mad Max' type of rush for resources. It was dangerous on many levels.

Inexperienced fuel raiders were caught well before they could jeopardize themselves or the local community members. They were told that the fuel was under pressure and had to be extracted by hand pumps now that there was no electricity to power the bowsers. They were told they would get a share of the fuel for their cars. Names were taken, addresses shared but no one had a phone number to ring to verify the promise. Thousands were given the same answer and eventually the fuel was secreted away in the deep dark of the night to a place where no one would dare to tread. Thousands of hectares of land were suddenly the addresses of thousands of abandoned car yards and airfields across the country, full of rusty and dusty machines that have no power to move anymore. What do you do with millions and millions of useless vehicles? Strip them down for raw materials like glass and leather seats. Make sculptures out of the suddenly still and statuesque heavy machinery bulldozers, backhoes and cranes. Steal whatever is left of the fuel to run a generator, shelter for the homeless, take the wheels off and make your own Earth Maggot powered vehicles, giant bicycles, a steam powered engine; but what for? Where do you travel to if you can? To see family of course and support each other during the technological un-renaissance; or build a vehicle that can carry large amounts of resources. Horses and camels are suddenly re-employed as beasts of burden to haul trailers and be bred for meat. All the delivery trucks in the world and their drivers are now obsolete. The new transport has gone back to the horse and cart and the camel train. There are no electric cars or scooters or anything else that requires a charged lithium battery to move. The batteries, however, can be annoyed, prompted, teased to produce some sort of heat energy so people start to collect them.

Wheels become valuable commodities and make-shift carts, like you've never seen in history books, evolve creatively to transport rocks, food, water, wood and building materials stripped from abandoned government structures. There's no one needed in those buildings anymore.

No phones or lights (a bit like Gilligan's Island) and millions of public servants unemployed and wondering where they are going to get a pub lunch special at 12:30 every week day. They will eventually become the customers to the farmer and his resources. But how will they pay, money is pointless, gold is more precious but suddenly devalued. They will have to work for their water and shelter and food. More farmers mean more food and more children fed. Populations move out of the barren city into the life-producing land where water is cleaner and more plentiful and nettle soup becomes a reality for an inexperienced hunter-gatherer family dinner.

Very soon, everything looks like food, trees and their fruit, frogs, caterpillars, grasshoppers and katydids and any non-carnivorous birds; even well-fed dogs come under the scrutiny of the always-hungry Earth Maggot. Cats and rats would be the ultimate emergency ration like in Russia during certain world wars. First the dogs disappeared, then the cats and then the rats. You knew you would be starving when there were no rats but us Earth Maggots are voracious and they turned their eye to the plumper of the maggots and became cannibalistic. How long would it take the 21st century maggot to go cannibal? How long could most people resist the urge to eat another Earth Maggot? Well, it's you or them. Your neighbours are barbecuing a fresh maggot leg next door and have invited you over to share in the juicy young shanks that they had legally procured and had basted in the finest left over sauces in their pantry. You refuse of course, wondering who the poor maggot was and the thought of eating a lower leg including the gastrocnemius and soleus muscles which would feed into the tough and unchewable Achilles tendon like on a lamb shank but slightly tougher. Then you smell the charcoal grilled marinated meat wafting over the fence and your hungry and suddenly vampiric wife says, "Oh come on, let's give it a go, how much different could it be? Just pretend it's lamb."

The farmer has fresh milk and can still make cheese and yoghurt. All these proteins become valuable food unless you can hunt your own protein or snare it. How much gold would you give a farmer for some milk and cheese everyday for your family? The shortage of fresh meat from cows and chickens has left the stranded Earth Maggots craving a good steak or some barbecued sausages. KFC is not available. There are still animals on the farm but they have become precious to ensure they are able to continue into the future. They are fed better than most Earth Maggots now and are the most sort after and expensive meat on the planet. Chickens are relatively easy to kill but if you want a steak you better be prepared to sacrifice a lot of your gold and be part of the slaughter of the beast. Nothing is wasted; fat, bones, offal, eyes and tongue, the rest goes to fertilize the vegetable garden. How would you slaughter your own beast that you had named 'Colin' without using a gun? After eating it would you need a 'Colin'oscopy? Also, how would you preserve the meat without refrigeration? Salt of course...

Now, if you could provide another source of protein, you would become an important contributor to the un-renaissance movement; let's say a hunter, trapper or a fisherman. Not too much technology needed to catch fish and there must be thousands of fully stocked BCF stores to provide everyone with a rod and reel and some hooks n lures n shit. Each to their own, but if you are clever you can catch more than you need and trade it for say a steak or a week's worth of fresh dairy. Just don't let it sit around for more than a few hours or it's fertilizer for your garden.

All the Earth Maggots will be seen at the beach or river or lake hoping to catch a feed and probably eating it on the spot once caught. What about wild birds? Does the protected species law to protect bin chickens suddenly disappear and they are fair game? They would be relatively easy to catch especially when there's a bunch of them honking in a tree. Just a big cast net would cover a dozen.

They taste like vulture 'apparently' which is a bit like turkey which is a bit like chicken I'm told. There are millions of these birds hanging around every dump in Australia. Rather than being a pest to humans and ecosystems they could become an instant source of protein to the suddenly very hungry Earth Maggots.

I think eventually the Ibis's will become wary of humans and move to less dangerous feeding grounds as dumps will disappear into the ground, schools will not have any rubbish bins for opportunistic scavengers and bin chickens may very well return to their status of 'Sacred Ibis' thriving in the tropical wetlands where no Earth Maggot has ever been.

No cars or machinery means a lot less emissions, the air is cleaner, plants begin to invade the spaces that Earth Maggots used to mow. The roads are being overgrown with grass and become walkways to nowhere. Those with garden tools and blades of some sort can control their environment, plant seeds, grow some of their food.

The people I asked initially don't want to know about that possibility. They don't want the world to go backwards because everything has become so easy in life that they don't have to think and they don't have to work. But here comes the wake up call. The world is going through a radical change, very fast and you may miss it if you are complacent, ignorant, slow witted or just determined not to learn what is real and emerging. No one wants to lose their first world privileges they have worked so hard to earn. No one wants to lose the benefits they have gained and then, a voice behind me scares me into reason. "If you ask this question then you must have an answer, even if it is your own." Yoda? I thought.

Unsurprisingly, it was the diminutive multi-instrumentalist sax-playing member of the original hypothetically questioned group whose name rhymed with that of a well known Japanese Anime character which sounded a bit like 'pick or choose'.

'Yes", I said definitively, "I have the answer, but you're not going to like it."

I focussed my gaze on her and answered confidently,

"I'm living in the present, I'm learning from the past and I'm thinking about the future. This has to be each person's mantra if the world is to survive." She nodded pretending she understood but I repeated it slowly anyway. I'm living in the present, I'm learning from the past and I'm thinking about the future. Those words mean nothing unless they are put into context.

There may not be another chance to consider the future for yourself because the future will decide what it wants to do with you. Choose carefully how you move forward.

It seems we'll all be blessed by the visit of the Bard
We will listen to the voice of the stories he tells
I know it's not easy as you compose, it's quite hard...
Like a stroll along a white beach collecting sea shells

Yet it all comes together at the end of the tale
And we reminisce about what might have gone before
Your imagination will undoubtedly set sail
As you search for pearls of wisdom on a distant shore

We did indeed have a visit from the Bard today
He shared stories of life, love and the absence of war
Entertaining and engaging, we laughed half the day
After the homework excuses I had a sore jaw

We dressed up as monkeys and wore funny coloured hats
And heard stories and poems from Aussies and ex-pats

And another thing, I've been wondering lately...........................

Some very realistic conversation starters.

- Climate Change Bullshitters.

- Cosmetics and fashion.

- The role reversal of pets.

- The power of media and social media.

- Dehumanizing people with lazy language
  (That and who, then and than, impordand and important)

- I'm rich; I really don't care if other people suffer.

- Waste is someone else's problem.

- When Phones, cars and computers are all voice activated.

- Musos vs. AI; live vs. Digital.

- Chat GPT in schools will dumb you down.

- Victims of our own systems, going too hard too fast.

- Could you grow / kill your own food?

- If you had to leave your house in ten minutes...
  all that you can't leave behind.

- What legacy do you leave your children / family?

- Illegal drugs of the 60's / 70's are now mainstream
  medicinal remedies.

- There are as many different versions of reality
  as there are people.

- Inter-subjective order dictates your reality if you let it.
  What is morality?

- What is your relationship with nature?

- All we have to do is just keep talking. (*Stephen Hawking*)

- Burn or bury your rubbish?

- Something's gotta change, everything must change.

- Claiming ignorance is no excuse.

- Boomers vs. Zoomers.

- Will future generations learn lessons from the stupid humans of the past or will they repeat them?

- Will future generations learn lessons from the clever humans of the past and capitalize on them?

- Greed vs. Wisdom.

- Would you really like to live to be 150?

- IS Q Anon real?

- Will the next generations be able to write with a pen?

- What do you think of compulsory conscription as a solution for the unrest of the hot youth?

- Is love real or is it just familiarity and comfort?

Thanks for reading, enjoy your coffee
and do something nice for someone every day.
Oh, and smile, it's infectious!

www.ingramcontent.com/pod-product-compliance
Lightning Source LLC
Chambersburg PA
CBHW072145130726
47909CB00004BB/1190